# Up The Way

### By
### Benjamin Janey

www.dcbookdiva.com
www.myspace.com/dcbookdivapublications

Published by DC Bookdiva Publications
Copyright © 2009 by Benjamin Janey

ISBN-10: 0615-23655-3
ISBN-13: 978-0-615-23655-1
Library of Congress Control Number: 2008941602

First Edition, April 2009
Printed in the United States of America

**Publisher's Note**

*This is a work of fiction. Any names historical events, real people, living and dead, or the locales are intended only to give the fiction a setting in historic reality. Other names, characters, places, businesses and incidents are either the product of the author's imagination or are used factiously, and their resemblance*, if any, to real life counterparts is entirely coincidental.

Cover Concept by: Tiah Short
Edited by: Dolly Lopez, L. Martin Pratt Johnson
Graphic Designer: Oddball Dsgn

**DC Bookdiva Publications**
#245 4401-A Connecticut Ave
NW, Washington, DC 20008
www.dcbookdiva.com
www.myspace.com/dcbookdivapublications

## *Dedication*

A very special dedication to my eldest daughter, Najah George. This first page represents my first step in the right direction. Thank you for allowing me back into your life.

Love,
*Daddy*

# A Promise Kept

My very first book I'd like to dedicate to Annie Lorine Allen, the wonderful mother of our two children. Thank you for sharing this dream years ago, and for all I've put you through, this is my sorry for 2009. Even though we're not together, why are we so far apart…?

To my son, Shekeem, and daughter, Shamik. You've made my life worth living, having been the glue to help me hold on to love when at times I didn't love myself.

Mae Harriet Janey, known to me simply as "Mom". Take a bow, because you deserve it. Thank you for having me, and I hope you'll be proud to witness that against all odds I've finally found myself.

Preston Price, you played a role in my life that reminded me today that "Dad" is a verb, and it's about what you did, not what you didn't do. Thank you especially for putting up my first basketball hoop, and although this isn't the NBA, we ballin'!

I have two of the best sisters in the world. They believed in me just because I'm their brother. Thanks, Chantel and Leslie! My Aunt Valerie has been a sister to me more so than an aunt. So, please accept this dedication, as well, because as doors open, we all can fit…

Also,

In loving memory of my grandparents, Herman and Ruby Watkins, my uncle Walter Watkins, his soul mate Mary Hunter, and their daughter (my cousin) Sonya "Pigeon" Watkins. And last but not least, my cousin Lisa Watkins. Rest in peace, Dwight Hooten.

Love you, Family,
*Bro. Benjamin*

# Acknowledgements

All praises due to Allah for blessing me with the ability to push my pen with authority. I thank Allah for allowing me to partake in the urban novel literary movement. A few words may be profane; however, I must speak today the language of the masses I've intended to reach. I write for the unlettered man and woman, just like the Good Shepherd came for the lost sheep. I pray that my sole intention to increase literacy participation is fulfilled, and may Allah accept my intention with just rewards.

I would like to thank Tiah Short and DC Bookdiva Publications, who saw me as a fallen star just needing the power to shine. Also, to all of you behind the scenes that helped to make this book possible. Although none of us have yet to meet in person, we all took it personally to let it do what it do! The world is your stage. I applaud you, so please take your bow. Dolly Lopez and Linda Williams, good lookin'!

Shout out to my niece, Cassie Wilcox. She's my vice-president for life. At thirteen and pretty swift with a pen, I'm expecting big things from her. Thank you for your love and support, because you and I kept dreaming until it came true.

To my youngest nephews, Dajai and Casson, I'm proud of the way you're both growing up into fine young men. Always make your next move your best move, and lead your own way so you'll end up where you want to be.

Also coming to the page, a big shout-out to my other two nephews getting their grown-man on, Mike and Cullen Mason, "reppin' the Gee" in Millville, New Jersey. We gonna get on it and do big things! Nothing is ever accomplished without a dream of something or someone better. Therefore, the only thing we quit is doing dumb shit.

Bro. Casey, the door is open to build another chapter in our lives. Bro. Captain (Keith) told us to make things happen, not wait for things to happen. He said, "Come on, brothers. Y'all got the damn teachings!" So fall in, sir, and let's move out. Stars shine brighter together.

To my uncles, (Herman, Jr.) Horace and Butch. See, everyone has a gift. It just took me longer to unwrap mine. I thank you in advance for helping me bring our family together. I may be the black sheep, but we come from the same flock, remember?

To the rest of my family and friends, I assure you life is a constant grind. I thank you all, because in some form or fashion, you were part of the thought process.

To "Ms. G." (Counselor J. Garris) and Lieutenant Bernard, both at New Haven County Correctional Center in New Haven. CT, I thank you for everything.

Nonetheless, I thank R&B for setting the mood; Hip-Hop for the creative attitude; and Reggae for setting me free.

Thank you all,
*Bro. Benjamin*

# Chapter One

Now here's a story. It's Friday, the first of October. I'm on a crowded city bus ready to do me. What better way to make moves than to be in the thick of things, ya heard?

My up-top attire had me looking like a youngin'. You know, my Eddie Bauer, a white T, my sagging jeans, and my crisp wheat Timbs. I had to sag with the matching fitted, while my ears and neckpiece gave haters the chills.

I guess jail does preserve a nigga, because I looked damn good for twenty-four. Plus, keeping up with my "gorilla" and not wearing the stress that meat gives you was a given. Real recognizes real, and hood niggas and bitches respected the "gorilla" because jail muscles for real, be having a brotha on swole, you feel me?

It seemed like just one of those days. The sun was shining, causing my light brown skin to glisten. The mailman was poppin' and the EBT bitches with their seeds were strollin' already. You see, at this time, the state and Feds were still in transition to make all funds electronically available. Therefore, on a day like today, the mailman was still "that nigga!"

My baby-momma called me early in the game. She was doing her first-of-the-month regular, wanting cash and flippin'. I was like, "Damn! I don't get a check!" Then I hit her with the usual, like a dummy. "Be easy. I gotta catch some sales first," I said.

Hell, that didn't fly too well, because she wasn't tryin' to hear shit. It was like the slightest thing sent her into flip-mode. She blew my phone up with, "I hope you die! You gonna go to jail, motherfucka!" She could even say all of this with one breath *and* include me going to hell!

I knew I shouldn't have answered the phone, but I'm damned if I do and damned if I don't. Until she gets dough, she'll hate to the extreme, telling my P.O. I don't live there with her, like that shit's funny – although I *don't* live there, you know.

I'm sayin' though, the bus was crowded. The hustlers were out today. You had the boosters with their foil-laced bags ready to hit the mall up. Since it's the first of the month, they'll be selling everything for at least half-price – but no more than 30% – because money was out there to get.

Then you got the "pick out the red card" nigga in the back of the bus. With cash in hand and imaginary velvet rope, his game would appear exclusive to VIP status. "Where is it? Where is it?" That's all you heard as he flipped and flopped three cards – two black and one red – doing his thing. The only winner for his sake would be his man that he has planted in the crowd. He was the decoy/hype man to get the game cookin'.

Always expect to see, "Oh, hell no " and his twin, "Can't get right" Their hook was, "Since you're peoples, you can buy brand-new jewelry 75% off the price tag or better." They had watches, rings, and chains that hung low. They were the first to have ice grills. One size fits all made it suspect. Everyone supported them because niggas be frontin'.

Now me, besides the business at hand, the bus gave me pleasure. There was always a cutie with a big fat booty. It was like heaven opened up for a minute. There she was, sitting there, with brown skin, brown eyes, and juicy-ass lips. I could tell she was sitting on a fat ass because her legs were the truth. Titties dead right and a little hairdo. "That's me, son!" I convinced myself.

The blinging from my chain and the sincerity of my gaze must have caught her attention. We exchanged smiles and I asked in my most seductive voice, "Ma, can I holla?"

She smiled and responded, "I might go to jail for messin' with you."

Wow! She really thought I was a youngin'. That book bag shit be working! I seized the moment and stepped to her. I kicked, "That's what's really good because I'm actually twenty-four, and that's how old I am and the hours in the day you got me open. Feel me?"

Pure radiance was revealed as she respected my swagger, responding, "Oh, really!"

We began small talk, as I stood over her trying to absorb her every word and heartbeat. With all the noise, I assumed she was talking about coming from a job interview and taking a physical. Once I heard the word "physical", in my mind, I began undressing her, forcing myself, however, to maintain. Real talk, *physical* was definitely a type of way I'd go real hard with her!

I added to the broken up conversation that I was off of work today, and what a lucky day for the both of us it had been, being that I had her undivided attention. I just had to mention that I'm into sales and plan to retire at the age of forty. Also, I was on my way from dropping my Benz off at the dealership to get it detailed and didn't need a loaner car because I'd be outdoors enjoying the nice weather today.

Main Street to the Ave. was guaranteed traffic. Then suddenly we were bumper-to-bumper at a standstill. That's when shorty noticed a roadblock ahead and flashing lights everywhere. I took a deep, hard swallow and eased my book bag next to her. As the police began to board the bus, I explained to her quickly that I may have a warrant for a parole violation, and for her to hold me down.

3

Now shorty was hood and understood without a whole big explanation. I eased away from her and the book bag, anticipating my turn to be quizzed for my government.

Sure enough, the detectives were looking for a purse-snatcher, while the patrolmen just fucked with anybody while trying to look official. Out of all the people on the bus, me and "Old School" had warrants and were escorted off to an awaiting cruiser.

I winked at shorty, blew her a kiss, and then off in the sled I went. It was a tight squeeze on the way to the North Pole (police station). To Old School it didn't seem to matter. He smelled drunk as hell anyway. Then it dawned on me. Yo, I didn't know shorty's name or nothin'! All I knew was that she was fine as hell with my three bricks of *yay*! This was some ugly math. Two years left on parole to serve minus three bricks of yay definitely equals a negative situation.

At Central Booking, it was the same old bullshit. One by one they called our names for mug shots, as if they didn't already have one on file. When it was my turn, I knew it was about to be a problem.

"Henry Roundtree," the officer called.

I didn't answer because that was my slave name my blessed name is Malik Muhammad. Most people including the police knew that the majority of South Jersey was God body and rid themselves of the burden of a slave name. Plus, with the tattooed star, crescent-seven, he knew to respect Malik Muhammad or get disrespected.

"Hey, Roundtree, your black ass ain't hear me call you, boy?"

As usual, I gave the officer-jackass just what he was looking for. "Fuck you, motherfucka! That ain't my got-damn name, and your mother didn't think I was a boy when I was fucking her white ass!"

Like clockwork, I'm maced, stripped naked, and placed in a dark-ass cell: for those who've been on lock, the "butt-naked cell". The strong scent of piss became the odor of the day. *What the fuck!* I thought, not giving a damn because those two years of parole were all mine to do.

True story, though, your conscience can be a bitch, because in my mind, I was on some "I should have reported to my PO" type of shit. Then again it was too late now. I planned on keeping it gangsta and wile-out for the next deuce.

It always killed me to see grown-ass men come to jail and then want to work and be good and shit. Fuck being good, I'm about to have me a good time. When it comes to cheddar, as long as they printing it, In or out I'm about getting it.

My eyes finally adjusted to the dark, with a slight sting from the mace. I relaxed my mind and thought about today's events and how it all unfolded. The three bricks were my future and the thought of shorty overwhelmed my present.

Although due to the fucked-up circumstances, just thinking about her got my dick hard. Being naked already, I figured, *what's the difference?* The reality is, within the next two years, I was going to beat my dick thinking about shorty. With no time like the present, I got it poppin'.

I could visualize shorty standing there, as I pulled her body next to mine. Caressing her thighs, I slid both hands under her skirt, gripping that firm ass. We kiss hungrily, her breasts tight against my chest, and her nipples poking through her blouse, harder than a motherfucka.

Laying back on the bed, I felt up her now entirely naked body, licked her toes one by one as an appetizer, slithering upward to part her thunder-thighs. Through her massiveness, I could see the moisture accumulating. Instinctively, she grabbed my head and began gyrating her hips to her own beat as her juicy mound embraced my tongue.

"Hey, boy, what in the hell are you doing? Don't be fuckin' jackin' off in here! This here is a police station, not up the way. According to this here paperwork," he said, waving his clipboard, "you'll have two damn years to choke your chicken. That's the problem with your kind now. Always horny, wanting to fuck something."

"Officer!" I yelled, as he threw me an orange jumpsuit through the bars and told me to put it on.

"What the fuck you want?" the officer yelled.

"Sir, I'd like to apologize for giving you such a hard time earlier. Could you please do me a favor?" I asked, sounding sincere.

"Boy, this better be good," said the officer.

"Oh, it is," I said. "Fuck you and go fuck yourself!"

The officer mumbled from his desk, "Fuck your one phone call…nigga!"

# Chapter Two

**Mia**

While walking a half a block from the bus stop, Mia replayed in her mind all that transpired. She thought she'd met the man of her hood dreams, because like most women, ain't nothing like a thug.

Then again, she felt like the little white bitch with the glasses from *Scooby Doo*. Mia had two mysteries to solve: One, she didn't know the nigga's name from the bus. Two, she didn't know what was in the book bag.

As Mia hurried up the driveway, she noticed both cars were gone, this was good sign indicating that no one was home yet. Eagerly she rushed into her room because whatever was in the book bag was killin' her. From reading so many urban novels, she hoped there were more than books in the bag. She could tell by the look on her homeboy's face when the police showed up that there probably were more than books inside.

As soon as she plopped her ass down on the bed and began to unzip the bag, her telephone rang.

"Hello."

"What's up, girl!"

"Hey, Jazz! I just walked in."

"Sounds like you were getting chased, breathing all hard and shit. So how do you think you did?"

Trying to sound professional, Mia answered, "Well, the physical part was rather simple being that I watch my carbs, exercise, and drink at least eight glasses of water daily. The mental is more of a hands-on approach and a reflection of ordinary street life. The majority of the men in prison are our people – straight hood, and that's all we fuckin' know."

They laughed.

Jazz and Mia were very compatible and resembled each other a lot. Both were fine, with a sense of humor. Each was elegant, with a touch of "get-ghetto" on demand. Jazz was twenty-four, two years Mia's senior, and in her heart considered Mia the little sister she never had. They've always been close since grade school, and Jazz even pulled a few strings to get Mia a job with her at the prison, the same shift and everything.

Again, Jazz had jokes, but could have been serious about some things on the low. Such as when she confessed to Mia on the telephone, "I've been working at the prison for almost two years now. The hardest thing for me is to stop fucking those fine-ass niggas locked up in there. You know a bitch get it in, and them *papi, Rico Suave* motherfuckas be getting blessed with this *chocha caliente de chocolate!*"

"Jazz, you ain't right!" Mia laughed.

"Mia, how that old song go? 'If fuckin' 'em is wrong, then I don't wanna be right'?"

"Oops! No you didn't! That's a Jazz remix, you think? Speaking of fine, though, Jazz, I was coming from the interview, and you know a bitch be busin' it. Anyways, a fine nigga got on. I thought he was in school because he had on new clothes and a book bag. You know how we used to rock our new school clothes in October because everybody else would've ran out of new shit by then. He said he's twenty-four, and he was on some fly shit like that's how many hours a day I got him open. Whatever! It was cute and I fell for it. He acted kind of thirsty, though, talking about, 'Ma, can I holla?'"

As if that was Jazz's cue, she said, "So much for education. What's his name, and where is he from?"

"Real talk, girl, fuck if I know, 'cause you won't believe the shit that happened."

"So you didn't get his name? Oh, my goodness!" Jazz responded, sounding like Sha-Neh-Neh from *Martin*.

"Girl, I'ma tell you, but for now, I'll just call him 'daddy'."

Getting all giggly and shit, Jazz was like, "You nasty trick! So what happened?"

"The police stopped the bus looking for a purse snatcher. The detectives got on, too, carding brothers, and two ended up with warrants. Knowing my fuckin' luck, my new daddy was one of them."

"How's he your new daddy and you don't even know his name?"

"Child, don't call it a comeback, but light-skinned brothers are back in season. The strangest thing, though, he purposely left his book bag, as if he wanted me to keep it."

"Damn, Mia! He probably was riding dirty. Did you check?" Then, "*Baru-u-u-u-p!*"

"Jazz, what da hell was that?" Mia asked, laughing hard as hell. "Please tell me that wasn't what I thought it was!"

Jazz starting laughing, too, and another one slipped out. "*Baru-u-p – Baru-u-u-u-p!*"

"Chile, them deviled eggs fucking with me. Go check the bag and call me back with the details. A job is a job, but the come-up is a payday, to-day! Oh, and speaking of riding, after working for a month or so at the prison, there's a way to get approved by the credit union for a brand new car."

"Holla!" Mia celebrated, while hanging up.

After getting off the phone with Jazz and the long bus trip, Mia had to piss her damn self. As she sat there on the toilet, just letting the piss ooze out, enjoying the relief she felt. She thought about her new daddy and how he undressed her with his eyes. She wondered where he wanted that kiss to land.

She was single, straight outta Jersey, but ain't had no dick in a New York minute. So just from wiping her pussy after pissin', she made a B-line for the bed, closed her room door, and locked it just in case someone came home. She then peeled off like a NASCAR – fast and with da speed! Her panties were soaked, and she could even smell her good pussy in the air. She was ready! The book bag had to wait.

Lying back on her fur bedspread, after tossing the book bag to the floor, she imagined her good fella watching her every move. With her mini-blinds shut and just a trace of daylight, her body promised a good show.

She licked her luscious lips very, very slowly. The slight draft from her ceiling fan caused her nipples to leave stab wounds in the air. Thick-ass legs wide the fuck open, she traced the sensitive lips of her soaking, hot, tight pussy. Gliding a finger deep inside, she began to fuck herself at a steady pace. Moans now escaping her, she added two more fingers and fucked her pussy for pain and pleasure.

Imagining he stood there stroking his swollen dick, they were both about to explode together. She screamed to him, "Look, daddy, look!" Shoving her middle finger in her asshole, she yelled, "I'm cum'in', daddy! I'm cum'in'!" He busted all over her body – no face or mouth yet – and definitely not on her fur bedspread.

The phone ringing brought her back to reality. She knew it was Jazz, with her shitty ass being nosey.

"Hello."

"Did you check?"

"No, Jazz, I'm about to now. I just finished."

"Finished what, Mia?"

"Nuttin'!"

Jazz thought this was a sarcastic reply. "How could you just finish nothing?"

"I didn't say nothing. I said *nuttin'*! Jazz, trust, this nigga got me on fire. I took a piss, and the next thing I knew, I was on the

bed butt-ass naked, fuckin' the shit out of myself. So I said *nuttin'.*
Feel me?"

"You's a freaky bitch, Mia!"

"Takes one to know one."

"Exactly! That's why we need a job being around the hardest
dicks in the state. No wonder all the bitches volunteer for overtime,
C.O. hoes. I'll volunteer, but I ain't around to be nobody's hoe. We
gotta be on some "bout it shit."

Mia finally opened the book bag. To her disappointment, it
contained a notebook with the star, moon, and seven, which
represented God body. Also three bibles, which didn't make sense,
A Quran maybe, but bibles? Hell naw! She leafed through the
notebook, trying to get a name or address, while Jazz waited at
bay. The notebook was a dead end, so she thought by removing the
bible's plastic wrapper there may just be a destination pre-stamped
and she could backtrack from there.

Carefully unsealing the plastic, the bible pages didn't open
like normal. The outside top cover slid back, revealing the makings
of a real ghetto story.

"Oh shit!" Mia screamed. "Come through. I can't say this shit
over the phone!"

"Say what?" Jazz echoed with the same level of excitement.

"I just said not on the phone! By the time you get here, I'll be
dressed. Hurry up, Jazz, 'cause you ain't gonna believe this shit!"

"Okay, one!"

"One!" And Mia hung up.

Meanwhile, she hid the one bible back in the book bag and
began opening the other two. Both also were jackpots. Nervously,
she put everything under her bed and went into her brother's room
in search of a cigarette. Mia was a nervous wreck and a 'Port
would calm her nerves. Don't get it twisted; Mia was hood and had
had her share of thugs. She also had an older brother aspiring to be
the next Nino Brown.

*I guess the old saying is true: Be careful what you wish for,*
she thought to herself, because just that morning she was hoping
for a come-up.

It wouldn't be long before Jazz arrived. Mia daydreamed of how things were about to change so dramatically for her. With a new well-paying job and dress code about to switch, "Every Day I'm Hustlin'" was about to become more than just a song to her. She could tell Jazz was down for whatever, and her brother needed no encouraging.

Mia already had a motto: "Always make your next move your best move.

# Chapter Three

### All That Shit

Some things never change. While turning down her music, Jazz pulled into the driveway, flipped open her cell phone, and voice-commanded, "Mia!" After the second ring, Mia answered and Jazz said, "What up, girl?"

Mia was like, "Please don't tell me! Please don't! I just know you're not out front calling instead of coming in."

Jazz just laughed and said, "Okay, I won't tell you," before disconnecting the call.

Mia opened the front door and waved her in. Locking the door quickly, they proceeded to the bedroom, where Mia pulled out the book bag and sat it gently on the bed as if it were full of explosives.

Jazz could hardly wait, unzipping the bag fast and pulling out...a bible, then another bible, a notebook, and another bible? She looked too through with Mia.

"Girl, I know you didn't gas me up to rush over here to see a Malcolm X starter kit! You could've told me on the phone your little new friend don't eat pork and prays all day," she said, referring to the notebook. "All that carrying on you were doing, I thought it was about to be some shit. Instead, you on the bus flirtin' with a miniature Farrakhan, wanna-be Jesse Jackson, in-the-news-ass Al Sharpton!"

Mia opened one of the bibles and showed Jazz what later weighed one kilo, and two more to keep it company. Even the notebook would come in handy for work, Jazz silently realized.

"Oh shit, Mia! It's three of them! We paid, girl! *We paid!* That's at least three bricks. Game da fuck over!" Jazz rejoiced.

Mia had to dull the moment, reminding Jazz that they were now both C.O.'s. However, she was already in another world. Jazz was on a New York shopping spree, bling-blingin'. She could see herself finally in official Prada, Gucci and strictly purple label. Mia, Jazz, and the "dark side" were about to become one.

"So, Mia, how we gonna do this?"

"I don't have a clue. Any suggestions?"

Jazz was always one to be their fearless leader and didn't mind adding her two cents to the matter. "I have an idea, but not certain about breaking it down, weighing, or cooking it up. Let's just stash it until after work tomorrow."

Being that the big day for Mia to start work was tomorrow, second shift is when it would go down. Jazz planned to ask around at work to get the lowdown on how to handle all of this. She figured who would better know than the convicts at work. Also, she had a secret or two to reveal eventually. One was the notebook.

Jazz had a foolproof method called "sex appeal". She'd ask a few O.G.'s the different weights and what made their product better than the next nigga's. A con's ego would kick in and they'd run their mouth all day.

*You know niggas in jail are long winded...talk a bitch to death,* she thought to herself.

"Mia, it wouldn't hurt to have your brother around, because he be posted up gettin' it," Jazz said.

It's just that all this time Fred thought neither of them knew his hustle.

"So, Jazz, do me a big, big favor. Since you live alone, why don't you take all of this shit and stash it at your place? Hell, you got a badge. Santa Claus ain't fuckin' with you."

"Okay, I'll hold it down; just keep it on the low. Oh, and who da fuck is Santa Claus?"

"Fuck around and get pulled over, you'll see them Christmas lights!" Mia laughed, relieved that Jazz would be pulling out of the yard with all that shit soon enough.

******

The next day came quick, while yesterday was still fresh in their minds. Jazz adopted an entire new persona once she entered the gates of hell at work. She went by the name of Ms. J., figuring an initial was safer than a first and last name.

Mia had to remember that from this point on, everything is real. She was assigned to view videos her entire shift. They ranged from previous riots to emergency medical situations. To her, that would be easy money for a day's work. However, she did kinda want to mingle with the men.

A portable monitor was set up inside the bubble (workstation), since the entire facility was on lockdown. The plexiglas station allowed her to see the entire tier and Jazz as she made her rounds.

The tiers and cellblocks were for more serious criminal offenses, such as violent crimes usually carrying a substantial amount of time. The dorms were a month-long orientation process as far as classification and mental health was concerned.

Ms. J. considered second shift to be her favorite because that's when the men worked out, showered, and flexed.

"Hey, Ms. J.!" Smitty yelled out.

A simple smile and wave always made his day. Smitty was a 'cane dealer finishing up a five year sentence. He would always flex his muscles to remind others that he was the king of their concrete jungle.

Jazz made a mental note to definitely holla at him in a few.

15

Tone was another favorite, except he didn't know whether he wanted to be a drug dealer or a pimp. He was amusing, but deadly. He was known for beating a couple of murder beefs.

"Got damn, Ms. J.!" he said, licking his lips and grabbing his nut sack.

*He knows damn well he could fuck me whenever—prison or not!* Jazz thought.

Tone was a pretty, yellow, "cock diesel" motherfucker.

"Tone, you got a minute?" Jazz lustfully called.

"All I got is time, my *hood McNugget*. What's good?"

Pouring on all of her charm, she purred, "Being that you're a baller, I want to know the in's and out's of the crack game."

She gave the reason that she was working on a project with her girls' group and needed street smarts instead of fake-ass theories from textbooks.

Tone felt flattered that she came to him out of all the niggas there and was sort of honored to be part of such great assistance. However, to keep his rep hood, he preferred to write down the game and pass it off to her before she went home.

Jazz loved his swagger and could barely control her smile.

Before she could leave, Tone hinted, "You know I gotta throw in a line for me and you."

"Play on, playa!" she grinned, slingin' her ass as she walked away.

Tone just grabbed his dick again and shook his head in adoration, imagining how he was gonna beat that pussy up.

When Jazz reached the bubble, she asked, "Mia, what's a *hood McNugget*?"

To her surprise, Mia had the answer because she heard it from her brother Fred. "A hood McNugget is tender brown meat requiring a human sauce, whereas McDevil's brag about tender white meat. Get it? I'm glad you're back, though, because I gotta piss like a racehorse. Where's the quickest spot?" Mia asked, while starting to do her "gotta piss bad" dance.

"Go down to Tier C to the end cell. It's empty and no one can see in there."

Mia wasn't shy, and off she went, not having time to look into cells or anything. Everyone was a big blur to her, yet a few men noticed a new "smell-good" in the air. It didn't take much to get a dick hard "up the way" she'd soon learn.

Upon entering the cell, she could see that it was spotless and definitely had a feminine touch to it. *Jazz must use this cell quite often,* she thought. The bed was neatly made and the mattress was plush as hell for jail.

Mia was startled by a woman's voice next door calling her and asking, "How you doin'?"

Being that after taking such a good piss put her in a playful mood, Mia said, "Wendy Williams, is that you?"

Getting her uniform back in order, she went to see who called her. She was shocked to see a light-skinned sexy bitch with titties and a fat ass, who had on tight biker shorts.

Trying not to look so surprised, Mia spoke. "Hello."

Brian knew he fooled her and ran with it. "Hi. My name is Brianna. You must be new," she said.

"Yeah, my first day. Are there any more women here besides you? Because I didn't realize this was co-ed."

"For now, I'm the only queen on this tier," Brianna boasted.

"Oh, the women are spread throughout the facility?" Mia asked dumbfoundedly.

Brian could not resist. "Oh, yeah, it's about ten of us. Do you have any eyeliner or lipstick you could spare? Chile, this Kool-Aid on my lips ain't cuttin' it. Lucky we're on lockdown, 'cause a sista cannot be seen wolfin', okay?"

Mia said, "On my lunch break I'll swing back through and touch you with something. By the way, I'm Ms. M. I'll holla," she said, heading back towards the bubble.

"Jazz!" she started in. "Why didn't you tell me this is a co-ed facility? I was taking a piss and heard a female voice speaking. I thought it was you, but I didn't hear any footsteps. Brianna is too fine to be behind somebody's bars." Mia went on, "I know they must keep her separated because niggas probably would take dat ass, word!"

Laughing hysterically, Jazz had to confess, but not until she had a little fun. "Chile, Brianna is a whole mess. Bitch stay in the mirror. I heard she suck a mean one, too, and will tell the business if you piss her off. I know she hit you up for makeup. Hoe probably got more shit in her cell than we got at home. Shit, niggas be fighting over that boy-pussy. Mia, you didn't know she was a *queen*?"

Mia, still in the dark, admitted that Brianna told her that she was a queen, and about ten more members of her crew were throughout the facility.

Then it dawned on Jazz. Mia must have thought "Latin Queen" not "*queen*" queen, as in balls and all. Still laughing, she let Mia in on the joke.

"Girl, Brianna is a nigga!" she confessed.

"Oh! I thought she was Latina," said Mia.

"No, Mia, you're not hearing me. I said Brianna is a nigga, like in balls and all. She meant queen like in 'Fairy Queen', not 'Dairy Queen', although that bitch wishes some milk came out of those sike-a-dillies. He cool, though – trust."

******

About two hours before shift change, Jazz stopped by Smitty's tier for the lowdown. "Hey, Mr. Smitty. I didn't forget about you. They got me training my homegirl today."

Smitty knew she needed information, and after such a boring day, he had jokey-jokes.

"So how are you today? Or better yet, how was your day?" Jazz asked.

"If you're gonna be in my dreams, not as good as my night," he answered with a devilish grin.

"Can I ask you a few questions before I go?"

Smitty eased off his bunk smoother than David Ruffin trying to take over the Temptations. Nigga had on some throwback gold silk boxers with matching BVD tee, a black suede smoking jacket that hung open, and a pair of black slip-on gators.

18

With too much style and grace for any one person, he finally responded, "Questions pertaining to? Because you know I don't be talking to the police. I came to jail with a 'Stop Snitchin'" white tee on. I'm gangsta – triple O.G. like if you see the police, warn-a-brotha. You heard Jeezy. 'Can't Stop the Snowman'. But off the record," he added, licking his lips, "Ms. J., you so fine I'd tell on my momma for a piece of that Kit-Kat bar. Watch out now!" he laughed, pointing both index fingers her way.

"That is it!" Jazz giggled. "I'm working on a project with my girls' group and need street credibility. I need to know in 'crack talk' what's a dime, twenty, a half and a bump, and how to spot undercovers. I need it all, Smitty."

"I gotcha, Ms. J., but with all that talking, you may have to slip a brother a cold soda or something," he said, with his eyes piercing through her uniform.

"Okay," she replied, "I'll get you the soda because I know your 'somethings' and I just got my hair did. Naw, boo-boo!" she said, while tapping her ass.

He talked fast and gave her plenty to try and retain for now. Also, she still had to scoop that kite from Tone.

True to his word, Tone threw in his lines first. "Ms. J., as I live to love you, smother me with your tenderness while I adore you from afar."

Now that hit Jazz right between the legs, getting moist in seconds. Thinking to herself, *Damn, jail do make some niggas poetic justice like a motherfucka! Tone gonna fuck around and hit this real soon, sexy yellow motherfucka!*

******

Finally, at the end of their shift, the ride home was kind of quiet, as if to save energy for tomorrow morning. Mia wondered to herself, and then aloud, "What if good fella comes back for his book bag?"

Jazz popped open her glove box, displaying her Nina Ross.

"Fuck 'im! Tell 'im you ain't got it. Tell 'im you left that shit on the bus. Hood rules apply. Mia, if you're scared, get a dog," Jazz teased.

\*\*\*\*\*\*

Jazz pulled up to Mia's house early the next day. Mia was finishing up her workout, which was a new thing because neither of them were morning people. Jazz began sharing the information accumulated, and they were now just anticipating Fred's grand entrance.

Mia's brother was definitely a "stunna". He couldn't even pull into his own yard without the music bangin' loud enough to wake up the dead, with the audacity to rep bad boys move in silence.

Fred was doing him, and still today, Jazz was moved by his presence. After all, he was now tall, brown-skinned, with shoulder-length dreads. He was between a Gold's Gym nigga and a true gorilla because he had never been up the way. But since he had peoples in and out that he worked out with, let's just say he got his 'monkey' on and would torture any woman by just removing his shirt, especially in the summer. He always dressed to impress and rocked the nickname "Escalade".

It seemed like money could make anyone look good. Ever since Fred got his lawsuit, he'd been ballin' real hard. While growing up, Mia, Jazz, and Fred went from being crying, snottynoses to ugly ducklings, and now swans. Fred was like the little drummer boy turned Dr. Dre beat. He was fine as hell. Yet, he was like Tommy from *Martin*… he didn't work. Often times, he acted like Goldie from *The Mac*.

As soon as he hugged his sister, he took Jazz into a hug, while gripping her ass cheeks hard like he wanted to pop 'em. On the low, Jazz loved it!

Mia took charge. "Fred, I'm glad you could make it this morning."

"I do still live here. It's just that dem hoes be tryin' to keep me," he bragged.

"Seriously, though, we have some important business to discuss."

In a panic, Fred began his questioning. "Is everything alright? How's Momma? You pregnant?"

Jazz blurted out, "Oh, it's good news...real good news."

Mia tossed him the book bag and he pulled out a bible, looking puzzled. "You got saved, or you're about to become a nun. Either way, y'all could've called me with that, ya heard?"

"Slide the cover back," Mia directed.

Following her instructions, Fred began his official journey to hell.

"Oh shit! Oh shit! That's what's up! Goddamn, that's what's up!" Reaching for the other two bibles, he began snatching the covers off, going deeper into excite-mode. "Oh shit! Oh shit! Say word! It's a wrap!"

They all embraced, solidifying their togetherness and joy.

Calming down slightly but talking a hundred-miles per hour, Fred asked, "Who got got?"

Jazz told him how Mia's game is so tight that a nigga on the bus got bagged and left the shit with her. The good part is they don't know each other from Adam.

Fred concluded by giving Jazz dap. "Hood rules!"

Mia was once again puzzled by the phrase. Not meaning to sound square, she had to ask, "What does 'hood rules' mean?"

Fred and Jazz both laughed while trying to explain. "Ain't no rules in the hood. It's all about fuck you, pay me," they mutually defined.

Fred thought Jazz's explanation as to how Mia ran across the product was missing something. Nevertheless, it didn't matter. "So, girl, what you gonna do with all that shit?"

Mia and Jazz both responded by doing a little dance. "Bling-bling!"

"You down, my nicca, or what?" Mia asked, smiling, so proud of herself to finally be able to look out for both Fred and Jazz for a change.

Fred just had to go into Mac-mode. "You see, baby, we gonna let it do what it do; make it rain and clear it out." Returning back to himself, he asked, "But who's the kid?"

Mia shouted, "'Hood rules, nicca!" feeling overly satisfied with her new slang, and causing a good laugh.

# Chapter Four

## The Bing

Malik was arraigned in court on Monday and sentenced on the spot. He accepted the two-year violation like the thoroughbred he was. Many men weren't built like that, because being sent back to San Dora wasn't a walk in the park.

San Dora was definitely the big house up the way. It mainly housed twenty-years or less, with the small exception of a few lifers. This was the range with too much negative energy to unleash still. In other words, you come in try'na fit in and leave out one of three ways: bitch, beast, or God-body.

Since Malik's original sentence was ten years, with violence, a pre-release facility was out of the question. At the age of sixteen, he was feared, and therefore tried as an adult.

Being no stranger to time, he got reacquainted with some of the Gods that same night. Orientation/mental health evaluation was dormitory style. Word of his return had reached before he did, setting the stage for a reunion.

Born Freedom was his man, and they rolled thick in the world and in the bing. Born Freedom had about two joints left to serve, so they took it as a sign to ride the two calendars out together.

Embracing, they greeted.

"Peace, God."

"Peace, peace."

Born, overwhelmed with his main man's presence, said, "Say, word is bond, you're only here for the violation?"

"Word is bond," Malik stated with a half-smile, knowing it could have been worse, like possession of three kilos with intent to sell—not to mention within 1,500 feet of a school. True story, anywhere a nigga tries to cash in tax free is 1,500 feet from some bullshit!

Malik and Born Freedom discussed on the phone last month about Malik's dirty urine sample. Malik went on to say, "Fam, I was burnin' it down in the world, melting piss cups like crazy. I drank that tea shit from the Rasta spot and took Golden Seals. Shit, I could'a copped a forty of piff and said 'Fuck it!' I was smoking lovely. Friday on the bus, I got bagged and had just met the woman of my dreams."

Staring into space, Born broke in. "So, how's the paper chase, God? I enjoyed the jelly on that bread, and my moms said you kept her right. That was real, peace."

Born Freedom was real with his, and Malik kept it tight when he was out. Malik's name rang with respect up the way, causing everyone, even the D.O.C., to feel some type of way.

"Well, you know we do what we do," Malik stated, embracing Born. "I'ma lay it down for tonight, and I'll see you at God-hour, family."

"True, salaam."

"Word, Ak' (ock)," as they parted.

Born turned to shout, "I got cake for oatmeal!" He was humoring himself and reminding Malik of their usual trade.

Malik didn't fall asleep right away. He still wondered how he was going to explain leaving three kilos on the bus with a shorty he didn't even know. Not that his word wasn't bond. It just didn't taste right saying some dumb shit like that, but better than catching a drug case.

He lit a cigarette and blew a couple of O's, wondering if he'd ever see shorty again. Malik was certain that she was from around the way. After all, she was on the bus headed to the hood. Fighting to keep from beatin' up again, he dozed off in hopes of sweet dreams.

"Allah-Akbar! Allah-Akbar! Allah-Akbar! Allah-Akbar!" the call to prayer wakes all the brothers. The Muslims are so deep that you got the Gods, Sunni, Shiite and the Nation, who at least peacefully pray together.

After prayer, "Chow time" is blared on the loud speakers to awaken the remainder of the population.

The Gods still had their same section in the chow hall, and it was like a big family reunion. There was practically a standing ovation when Malik approached the table. Every one was more interested in Malik's episodes in the world rather than breakfast. However, Born Freedom could sense something was wrong with Malik.

Being the head tier man, Born Freedom could pretty much move around the entire jail without a problem. The most work he'd do was buff the main hallway and then post up by the visiting room, seeing what extras he could get plugged in with.

The C.O.'s were like night and day. Some wished they could have been police, and some just got a paycheck and wished to go home in one piece. Like anywhere, they had their own cliques, and one crew was always with the bullshit.

While in the streets, Malik had heard about this not-so-discreet group of bitches, and how one gay convict got down. They called him Brianna aka, Brian, and how he acted just like a bitch. He heard that Brian talked a good game and for no price, he was fucking or sucking, whereas Ms. J. and the other C.O. bitches had niggas ready to hang-up over that pussy and concentration (head).

Lunch was at "Knowledge-knowledge" and first rec was at Knowledge hour. They all agreed to meet and discuss operations. Born had juice, so he'd go get Malik from the dorm.

"What's troubling you, God?" Born asked.

Without hesitation, Malik said, "I left three bricks with shorty on the bus and I don't even know her math."

"Say word!" Born said, adding drama to the matter.

"Word," Malik continued. "It's nothing. Shorty's hood, and everyone knows three of them thangs is enough to get your wig split."

Born tried to make light of the situation by reminding Malik that it would be about a deuce exactly before splitting any wigs, especially without a name. "You might get to smack off a kuffi in the meantime, but it's nothing. As long as they printing it, we gonna be getting it. No doubt!"

At the meeting, records reflected that money was still being made. The demand had finally become greater than their original supply. Actually, this was why Malik had stepped up their weight for the first of the month.

Don't get it confused; there was money on the brick to make, yet the profits quadrupled in the bing. In addition, there was really no getting caught because you're already in jail. At least with their operation, it appeared foolproof.

Keeping the cipher complete, once the brothers learned of the unfortunate circumstances, it was all love.

Akbar, another head of the Gods said, "No need to cry over spilt bricks." This got a laugh. "We have enough dough to buy at least one brick right now. That's not even counting our own stash, because in here, we're either stuffin' or trickin' dough."

So all and all, it was about a three-day setback, and who in jail hadn't learned patience, if nothing else.

Back to Akbar, he was wild with his. He'd been down for a decade and some change on a half a deck (26) *'til* ever! You know, Bernie Mac said, "You know it's a long time when you take the *'for'* out that motherfucka!"

Ak' had a white C.O. making hella-moves for the Gods. Although she was a devil, the white C.O. bitch was thick up like whoa! Everyone knew Akbar was smashin' it on the low. They just didn't want to fuck up his Muslim. After all, he arranged shit, it was done, and everybody was paid.

The setup was pretty much the same as it was before Malik left. Any new C.O.'s were no business of the Gods, and vice-versa.

Brian was ideal, they both agreed, because the male correctional officers never searched him, and he actually said he knew the warden's son who probably was gay, too. Brian did receive special privileges for services rendered, such as a thousand dollars per week, which he wired to an offshore account. He also received street food, safety, and a cell phone. Everything remained on a need-to-know basis.

It dawned on Born to mention while he and Malik were walking the track, "Yo, remember that new C.O. that started just before you left named Ms. J.?"

"Oh, yeah, little her. She was dead right," recalled Malik.

"Well, she still is dead right, and oh, I think she likes me. Oh, I think she likes me!"

"Yo, Born, what you done turned into, a fan of dem Franchise Boys? Next thing you're gonna tell me she wanna lean with it, rock with it! Word, you need some double-A, air and ass, my brother."

"Real talk, Malik, you know while you were out in the world that the God was in here going real hard. I think Ms. J. down with the white bitch Akbar fuckin', because lately she's been friendlier than a motherfucka.

"Well, you know how shower time, after we get it in with the weights," Born continued, "the God be all swole and shit. I'm in my house (cell) oiling up my diesel, and she walks down the tier as if she was timing me."

Malik interrupted. "You need double-A, family."

"No! Peep the fly shit. She stopped right there in front of me," Born said, demonstrating she was not even an arm's length away from him, "And checked the God. You know I'm a gorilla and let my vine swing for her. Shit, her mouth dropped to the floor and she been on it ever since."

So, Ms. J. knows we're getting paper in here?" Malik questioned.

"Quiet as it's kept, she's hood, 'cause some clown came through that used to live around her way. They shipped his ass out of here with the speed."

"I appreciate all that, but does she know?" Malik insisted.

Born plainly said, "It ain't hard to tell. Birds of a feather flock together!"

Malik began making mental notes to himself regarding all that was gathered today. Akbar and Born Freedom were definitely thinking with their dicks. Both were slippin' on their pimpin', trying to make C.O.'s into housewives.

For confirmation, he asked Born, "Let me get this straight. I know there's more than two C.O.'s down: some fuckin' for a fee and some just straight get paper with Akbar's white bitch. And now there's Ms. J. My thing is I'm not concerned with their team. The key to our longevity is how many of them know about us. Feel me?

"I was in the world about a year and some change, come back, and my people's wildin out'," Malik went on. "Akbar broke the cipher, fuckin' with Snow White, and I bet he's rippin' that devil raw. You, Born, done turned into a got-damn stripper for Ms. J. Did ya rip yet, or just thought about getting some?"

Giving dap and throwing his hands in the air, Malik concluded, "Let it be known, it is the paper chase…the bing!"

Going separate ways, Malik decided on the last laugh today. "Born!" he called. "Shorty on the bus reminds me of Ms. J. come to think of it."

Born pumped his brakes. "Negative, my dude! Don't even try to skeet to mine. I'ma pay for that pussy! Get your own!"

28

# Chapter Five

## The Master Plan

Fred was up earlier than usual. He wanted to go chef up four-and-a-half and put it into motion. Mia and Jazz wouldn't be up yet to further discuss operations, and since Fred considered himself a "beast", he had a "monster plan" versus their "master plan".

He was at the head shop as soon as the doors opened, picking up red and pink plastic baggies. The red would represent his twenty pieces, and the pink would be for the girls' dimes. Jazz and Mia would need their own scales, so he grabbed two digitals and a box of razor blades and approached the counter.

Being a typical drug dealer, while the cashier rang up the items, he pulled out a "Chinese" bankroll, stuntin'. She commented, but not like he possibly hoped.

"I see you're still on the come-up," she laughed.

He stammered out, while tightly clutching his bag, "Fuck you, bitch!" and tossed two one-hundred dollar bills on the counter. In other words, he left her a sixty-dollar tip.

"You can fuck me once you get your weight up, Freddie!"

she responded.

Now that burnt Fred's ass up! But he refused to let what he thought was a minimum-wage chick fuck up his flow that day. The sun was out and he was still ahead of schedule, so he decided a quick car wash would do the trick.

Pulling up to The Water bumpin' Cassidy's classic "I'ma Hustler", his presence had to be known. All the morning playas were out to get their shine, and like a thief in the night, Fred stole a lot of niggas' thunder. Exiting his whip was like the show of all shows. Hydros dropped half a foot, sittin' on 30's, Crayola and chrome, while the doors cart-wheeled under midnight blue paint with silver metallic freckles.

Acknowledging his audience, pointing to his rims still spinning and looking like a kaleidoscope, he taunted, "You gotta love that!"

The dealers hardly ever washed their own cars, and Fred couldn't remember the last time his truck was dirty. Normally, a worker would wash their dealer's car or there'd be someone at The Wash trying to make it happen.

At this point, Fred didn't have workers, but with his new access to major weight, he knew he was due. Today was going to be the day because the come-up had arrived.

"What up, fool?" City yelled to Fred. "What you about to do? Wash your people's Escalade and take it straight back?" he said, trying to get a laugh.

There were a few chuckles coming from the haters, mainly City's crew.

Fred was getting heated. He knew City was a big, black roebuck nigga, fresh out the bing from a five year bid . Now this motherfucker must have really had "gorilla" in his blood.

Fred thought to himself, *City is the one frontin', because he worked for his connect and I just had to remind him.*

"Whatever, looking like a black-ass Deebo!" Fred said back, even getting a laugh out of City's people. He went on, "I know you get money, big piggy-bank-head motherfucka!"

That brought roars of laughter from the crowd, pissing City

off. Fred wasn't done, though.

"Look at that big-ass vein about to pop out your head, looking just like your mom with her wig off, playin' gangsta dress-up."

That did it, because City went "Ja-fakin'". "Blood clot! You naw no me star! Me x ur ras clot boy! Ya naw speak upon my mudda dem, shea gon a-ready wit' de fadda, Jah! Rastafaria, sien. Me naw play your lickle joke business and ray-ray! Ya wanfe dead!"

City was being restrained by some of his crew, while Fred grabbed at his waistline, indicating he was strapped.

"Damn, son! My bad!" Fred said, as if being apologetic. Yet his concluding remark was, "Shabba!"

In the midst of their verbal assault, Fred was scanning The Wash looking for a "do-boy". A do-boy was a nigga you tell what to do, and they do it. They don't really work for you, as in a crew or unit. However, based on their performance, they're viewed closely for potential.

Bingo! Fred spotted a new face and leapt at the opportunity to floss a little bit.

"Son! Son! Yo-yo!" he said, finally catching the new guy's attention. "You working or not?" he asked, flashing the Chinese bankroll once again.

The guy walked over and Fred put him to work immediately buffing the rims on an already clean truck. Sizing him up, Fred thought he was a strong looking crackhead and then cancelled that thought. The two teardrops on his left cheek represented some West Coast shit, and this nigga was either just new or on the run. Regardless, Fred was determined to make this new face crew.

"So, son, I'm Escalade. What it do, man?"

"I'm Douglas," the guy replied as he shined away on the 30-inch chromes.

"Douglas, you new around here?" Escalade quizzed, trying to pick up an accent. "The reason why I'm asking is because I never saw you around and I'm deep in the streets. Like see that big black motherfucka? That's City and some of his bitch-ass crew. He

31

works for his connect. After today, though, I'm going to be the connect and show niggas what's really hood. Now you are a grown-ass man, and I can dig washing cars is an honest day's work. However, 'round here you can't get no bad-ass bitches by washing cars, fool. Where you from, D.B.? Idaho? Because overalls been out."

"How did you guess? It must was my accent. D.B.? Why did you call me that?"

"I'm about to put you on my team, son, and you can't be rollin' with me and me calling you 'Douglas'. Shit, only family and a few good hoes call me Fred. Smell me?"

"So what's D.B.?" Douglas insisted.

"It's short for Do-Boy. You ain't up on Do-Boy?"

"Naw," Douglas said, purposely sounding country as hell.

"See, I knew you was an old Idaho-ass nigga, D.B. You in?"

Clueless, Douglas asked, "In for what?"

"Damn, Do-Boy!" Fred screamed disgustedly. "What do you think all these niggas do out here? We get it in. I know you tired of trying to outrun the poor house. You need to get on this paper chase. Roll with or roll out, nigga!"

D.B. didn't hesitate and gave Fred dap while grinning. "Yabba-dabba-doo!" D.B. yelled, causing their first of many laughs together.

******

Fred explained to D.B. that he had a few moves to make since it was still morning and they'd get back up around three. He gave D.B. his cell number plus 200 dollars, and told him to holla back at three o'clock so he could scoop him. Both guys parted happy, neither believing how easy the drug game's door was about to opened.

Finally reaching Jazz's house, Fred brought in the equipment he just purchased and headed straight for the kitchen. The girls gathered around, silently observing and absorbing all that they could. Like surgery, Fred began to operate.

"Jazz, I need the baking soda and a clean jar. Mia, hand me that bag I brought in. Here, everyone put these face masks and

32

latex gloves on."

Delegating like a true drug lord, he rattled in the cabinets in search of just the right pot and plates to make it happen. Adding humor as usual, using an infamous line from the movie *Scarface*, Fred said, talking to no one in particular, "Chi-Chi, get the Yayo!"

Mia brought out one bird as Fred covered the plate with plastic before placing it upon it. Unwrapping just a corner and chipping away one nice chunk, he had his two novices in awe, as if this was the norm for him. Quickly rewrapping the corner and taping it, Mia returned it to the stash.

Next, he plopped the corner onto the scale, demonstrating how easy it was to get a reading. He compared the functions to be similar to operating a calculator.

"Ah, perfect! Four and a half ounces," Fred said, knowing he was off by at least twenty grams over.

It's just that part of his "monster plan" was to appear accustomed to this level of hustlin' and lead the way. Fred only wished he was a beast.

While the pot on the stove started coming to a boil, Fred turned on the range fan and the other eye of the stove to begin frying onions for aroma purposes. He divided the "raw" into four chunks and sank one at a time into the jar half-filled with Wrey and Nephews (whites). Once the "kane" came to an oil form, he began whipping it up. He exaggerated his wrist motions, creating the illusion of his expertise.

The captive audience was amazed because neither had actually seen kane rocked up before. Three more times he repeated the cooking show, setting each boulder on a towel to dry. Now to formally introduce his "monster plan" (although the girls had plans of their own; Mia just didn't know it yet).

"Here's the deal. I figured since we have so much to work with, we must increase our demand. By switching up the game, we'd have everyone's clientele in no time. If we take a twenty piece," he said, holding up a chip off a boulder, "and sell it for a dime, it will be a wrap. Plus, I got a new worker who'll be serving all the new faces, so I won't have to worry about Santa Claus."

"I got here red bags and pink. I figured since the pink bags would be new to the area, they could represent both of you and the new deal. The red bags I'd use to serve my regular customers who spend twenty or better. So, the bottom line would be to sell carefully, but also as fast as possible. We can chip in and pay the help weekly based on his performance. I think Do-Boy will do just fine."

Just as Fred expected, the "monster plan" went well. However, Jazz felt it was time.

Clearing her throat and capturing their undivided attention, she said, "Mia, Fred, you're both family to me and everyone has a right to a secret or two. Just like we been knew you sold drugs, Fred. We just never questioned you because you're your own man. And Mia, we're only two years apart, and that baby sister I never had. What I'm about to tell you is kind of hard, so let's just say for now, the less you know, the better off we'll all be.

"Financially, ever since becoming a C.O., my whole life has changed. Mia, like how I told you after a month the credit union financed my car loan. Well, that was sort of the truth.

"At work," Jazz continued, "I hooked up with this ghetto white chick called 'Snow White'. She fucks with a nigga locked up there, and they be making moves. I mean major moves, and not no ounces of weed or cell phone bullshit. I'm talking 'Big-8's" or better each move. I do my part and get paid. End of story!

"But now since we have so much weight, I'm sure with the right inside connect we could expand and have the white bitch, I mean Snow White, working for us in no time. After all, she's dumb as hell and in it more for the dick than anything else," she said, ending her confession.

Everyone was shocked after that breaking news. Jazz's plan was brilliant, also. For now, they'd go with the "master plan" until Jazz put her hook into a new fish. Mia just had to play innocent and learn fast.

The clock was ticking and the girls wanted to at least get in a two-hour nap. They assured Fred that they'd learn more cuts next time, because the only dime and twenty they wanted to see was in their dreams.

******

With a new sense of power and money to be made, Escalade was about to become his own nemesis…"Captain-Save-A-Hoe!"

Rollin' down the avenue checkin' out the grown and sexy, the vibration of his cell phone brought him back to reality. A blocked call appeared on the screen, yet he figured he wasn't hot yet and answered.

"Yo, what it do?"

"Hey, Fred – Oh! I mean Escalade. Dis D.B."

"Yeah, nigga, shoutin' out my government!"

"My bad. You around?"

"Like clockwork. Where you?"

"I'll be at the spot in five minutes."

"What spot? Fool, we ain't got no spot!"

"Where we met at earlier and I put that work in for you."

"Oh, The Wash, right?"

"Yeah."

"Shit, nigga, you talking about that work you put in for me. I was about to hang this bitch up because you talkin' reckless like you suspect."

"From Idaho?" D.B. raised the question, as if to say, 'how could that be?'

## Chapter Six

### Mia's Observation

Excited about starting officially because the lockdown was over, Mia made sure her uniform fit like a glove. She even thought to herself how the color black accented her brown skin very well and how cute the boots looked on her tiny feet, as she pranced in front of the mirror complimenting herself.

Using the buddy-buddy system, she'd shadow Jazz's every move today to see firsthand how it was done. The main thing was to get the count right, because one error would throw the entire facility in a loop.

On their way to work, the air was confusing inside the vehicle. Jazz mentioned how it smelled like they were going to a club, not to work in a prison.

"Damn, Mia! What, you wasted the bottle?"

"Jazz, I know you ain't try'na get on me with that loud shit you got on, smellin' like a Glade Plug-in!" Mia laughed.

"You got me on that one!" Jazz had to admit.

Today would be quite informative for Mia. She'd get to see

who Snow White was and all the niggas worth fuckin'. After all, she was backed up and 'bout it!'

"'For now, we'll be in the cellblocks for ninety days. Once you complete your self-defense training, we'll be able to rove all over," Jazz said.

Mia defended, "I'm not scared of no nigga!"

"It ain't about being afraid. These are some of the biggest and baddest niggas on earth. These some real G's. They ain't no wankstas. Try not to lead them on unless you plan on fuckin' 'em for real. They respect that better," Jazz concluded.

To Mia, it still seemed rather quiet compared to what she expected. There was no roll call; they just punched in and headed to their assigned post. After changing command, they headed out for their first tier walk.

Jazz explained how it was just to familiarize themselves with the day's tone and observe body language to see if any unusual tension existed, and also to make sure none of the prisoners were harming themselves.

Mia did recall from the videos she watched the previous day how an inmate hung himself from the bars with a sheet. This is why every fifteen minutes a tour was done, because it gave better odds for a rescue attempt and prevention.

Ms. J. was like a superstar in the bing. Men, after hearing her keys rattle, looked forward to a woman's presence. Finally, the pleasant smells of two perfumes were getting a lot of attention. You could hear the mirrors sliding out of the bars so they could get a continued view after the C.O.'s passed by. The admiration could be heard.

"Damn! Look at dat ass! Two nice asses at that! I must be fuckin' dreamin'," was all you heard from the men.

They both smiled, swinging their asses even harder like video hoes. The good thing was, for the men, they had to walk back by because the tiers were dead ends.

Now remember, Born Freedom was on the tiers, and once he spotted Ms. J. coming, he greeted, "Hello, Ms. J., and hello... um?"

"Mia Short," said Mia, as Jazz corrected her immediately.

"Call her 'Ms. M.'. She's a new jack, but also my homegirl, so be easy."

Born Freedom took heed, flexin' his chest as much as possible.

As they walked away, Ms. J. commented, "And put a shirt on…showing off my stuff!"

You could hear the joy in Born's response, "I know that's right!"

Giggling like two around-the-way girls, Jazz schooled Mia to never give out her government unless she wanted to receive about a thousand porn letters in the mail from those niggas. Mia just had to keep in mind that they were criminals, and with the least amount of information, such as your full name, they could find out anything and everything about you.

Mia asked about Born Freedom, due to the comment Jazz made about "showing off her stuff". Jazz told her that he gets money with the Gods, and his boy, Akbar, was the one fuckin' Snow White.

"Jazz, he's built like a brick shithouse! I guess all there is to do in here is work the fuck out," Mia reasoned aloud.

Jokingly, yet dead serious, Jazz's replied, "Girl, we need to be out by the front gate waiting for these gorillas to come out. I could make a porno up in this bitch called *Gorillas Gone Wild!*"

*I bet it's some freaky-ass niggas up in here,* Mia imagined, feeling a little warmth in her sensual place.

In the break room, Jazz introduced Mia to some of her new fellow co-workers. Mia didn't recognize anyone from her self-defense class. Then again, the prison system was large in New Jersey. Based on the previous description and the two sellouts flocking around her, Mia had to give credit where credit was due. To her surprise, she even felt a twitch of sensation as she looked on thinking, *Damn, Snow White thicker than a muthafucka! I see why niggas try'na holla!*

Jazz introduced the two, and to Mia's amazement, *everyone* really called her "Snow White". Their handshake was warm, and

38

the eye contact and body language was there. Secretly, Mia was taken by the chemistry because she'd never been so attracted to a woman.

As the break ended just as quickly as it started, they all headed back to their assigned posts.

Back at the bubble, Mia sat, reviewing the rules and regulations, while Jazz excused herself, heading back down the tier to execute their plan.

Born Freedom was waiting, and after seeing she was alone through his mirror, he quickly stripped down to his boxers.

"I should have known!" teased Ms. J.

Born Freedom stood there semi-erect, as if this was their usual. His well-moisturized body and the flexing were taking its toll on her, but she had to complete her mission. Now was the perfect time because everyone was locked up until last chow.

Putting on her charm, and in a very seductive voice, she asked, "Excited to see me?"

The scent of her Victoria was no longer a Secret, causing him to go from semi to full-bone. Moving closer to the bars, she reached inside, grabbing a handful with plenty to spare.

With a slight moan, he asked, "Does she know about us?" referring to Mia.

"I did mention that I had my eyes on you," she blushingly confessed.

At the moment, it appeared to be more than her eyes on him.

He whispered, "So what can I do for you?"

Jazz said, "A little business and a whole lot of pleasure."

She licked her lips to reinforce "pleasure". Born was all set by now, thinking with his dick.

Jazz broke down the proposition, which was an offer that felt so good there'd be no refusing. While stroking and sucking at a steady pace, she mentioned that she had a friend that would front a key of kane to her with no interest for thirty days.

At a time like this, Born knew that was a great deal, because they could flip that at least three times and quadruple the dollar amount with each flip by then. He liked those numbers almost as much as he enjoyed the cum skeeting on the floor in front of them.

Trying to catch his breath, he said that he'd run it by his peeps, and for her to check back tomorrow.

Jazz had a better idea. She told Born she already knew about Akbar and Snow White, but figured why not sit on their kane and move the new shit first, start running things and still come off with the normal move, too. Eventually, they would have Snow White and the other C.O. bitches on their team put in the work.

Playing on Born's intelligence, by using the words "us" and "we", he interpreted Jazz and he to be a couple. (Dick thinking, as planned!)

On Jazz's return to Mia, she had a big smile on her face, indicating so far so good. Mia couldn't see what she had been doing nor hear the occasional sucks because of the distance and angle, but she could imagine.

To Jazz's surprise, she noticed Snow White walking away.

Jazz started in. "Oh, I see you bitches getting along!"

Mia explained that Snow White was a rover today and was just passing through. "She seems pretty friendly. We exchanged numbers, and she said she would give me a call this weekend."

Jazz warned Mia to be careful because Snow White might go both ways.

Defensively, Mia stated, "I'm strictly dickly!" knowing this may be the first time she lied to herself.

On the ride home, Jazz gave Mia the rundown on how things went with Born Freedom. Holding nothing back, she explained how she had him thinking with his dick, and that it would be on and poppin' for real soon.

"The leash is on that nigga's neck for sure," she continued. "After the hand-job I gave him and that big-ass nut he busted, I bet he's sleep, already dreaming about this good pussy!"

"Too much information!" Mia laughed, while waving goodnight as she went in the house, thinking to herself, *Jazz probably sucked his dick!*

# Chapter Seven

## The Takeover

Fred and Douglas, AKA Escalade and D.B., linked up and rode around scoping things out. Fred schooled him on how New Jersey streets were faster than in Idaho. However, D.B. never actually *said* he was from Idaho. Fred gave him that, and he just ran with it, being sarcastic.

The pink bags would be D.B.'s to move because there were always more dime sales than twenties. Crackheads get change before they come. It must be part of their ritual, getting "geeked" to keep coming back and forth instead of just buying it all at once.

Escalade explained to D.B. that he'd get paid on Saturdays like a real job, based on his performance. Plus, he'd get a bonus upfront to step up his wardrobe and get a "chop" (haircut). He couldn't stress enough the importance of a fresh cut to accentuate one's image.

Posting up on the One Way was the best strategy, Fred thought. Being in the middle of the block gave you valuable time to escape and see harm coming. Banging the music let the potential customers know it was on and poppin'.

Instructing D.B. to open his door because he was going to have to jump out and serve the customers immediately put him in the game. Fred knew it would be essential to their success for the people to learn his face fast, and the sooner the better.

Like clockwork, people began to swarm once they heard and saw the size of their dimes. Just as planned, it was only a matter of time before they would take over the hood.

In less than six hours, Fred sold out, thanks to D.B. He realized that he'd need more on standby at the lab for days like this, and better ones to come. Not once has he ever "rinsed" (sold) so fast. He figured somebody had to be missing money today.

Just as they headed off the One Way, City pulled up, feeling some type of way. It wasn't hard to tell he was tight!

"Yo, punk!" City yelled. "You and your boy think shit sweet? I heard y'all niggas sellin' boulders for dimes. Now you know that's fuckin' with my paper. I should jump out the car and fuck both y'all niggas up!"

With all the commotion, a small crowd gathered.

Fred was no Mike Tyson or the brightest bulb in the chandelier. Without really thinking, he screamed on City. "Fuck you, son! This is big business over here. You're like a K-Mart fuckin' with a Wal-Mart!"

He got some laughs from the crowd.

By the time City slammed his car into park and attempted to jump out, it was too late. Without notice, D.B. jumped out of the Escalade with his 40-cal., ready to handle.

Taking charge, D.B. checked the hell out of City. "What, nigga! What! Jump your big ass into one of these hot ones. Have your ass leaking. We do what we do, ya heard!"

Almost speechless, City questioned, "Where you from, fool, and who the fuck are you?"

Thinking fast, D.B. said, "I'm from Idaho, and I'm Do Boy. You ever fuck with dis nigga," pointing to Escalade, "me and my team will see you!"

Feeling himself, D.B. continued on, walking over to City and pointing the 40-cal. "Motherfucka, you got bank?" he demanded. "Get your big, black ass out the car! Run your pockets!"

He hit City with a slap shot, where you slapped and pulled the trigger at the same time. The gunshot scared the piss out of City, and everyone else for that matter.

D.B. took the money and threw it into the crowd, telling them that tomorrow's a new day. After kicking City dead square in his ass, he hopped back in the Escalade, calling City a "Sponge Bob Wet Pants ass nigga!" as Fred peeled off, making their exit more dramatic and hilarious.

Fred was really shaken half to death. Not wanting D.B. to notice, he said, "Damn, Do Boy! They got some crazy niggas out in Idaho, I see. That shit was real gangsta. Where did you learn that shit from? Real talk, you got us mad props. That nigga City really pissed himself. The only thing now is we got beef like a motherfucka!"

"The mo-money the mo-problems. Fuck it!" D.B. said. "If need be, I have heat holders that bust their guns. City don't want to die. We just gonna have to keep him from pissin' on himself and feed the nigga once we take over. After all, he's a big boy — fool's gotta eat!"

First stop, Fred hit the liquor store and grabbed a half-pint of "Hen" to ease his mind.

Then D.B. copped a 'fit for the next day. He felt he deserved it or an Oscar. Douglas definitely had to replay this day for sure, and figure out how to handle City without killing him.

# Chapter Eight

## The Gathering

By 7 A.M., Fred and Mia arrived at Jazz's place ready to get busy. Jazz had all the essential tools set out, enabling Fred to begin at once.

The girls began snappin' the tiny plastic baggies open, eventually catching on to the technique, just like poppin' your fingers.

Jazz mentioned to Fred that she'd know by the end of the night how much Mia and she would need for the bing, and how much of it was to be cooked up and how much powder.

Fred just nodded in agreement, focusing like a chemist hard at work. Once he set the kane out to dry, he could hardly wait to tell of his adventures yesterday.

Dumping a brown lunch bag full of cash on the table, Fred welcomed the girls to the big leagues. He boasted on how he sold out in six hours, and D.B. had control of the hand-to-hand transactions. He didn't mention the drama with City because he knew they would worry too much, although he was a little shook himself.

They stuffed the bags, getting the hang of things rather quickly, and Fred was out of there by 10 A.M.

Mia had brought her things with her for work and headed straight for the sofa, leaving Jazz to clean the kitchen all by her lonesome. Jazz was tickled to see how cute Mia looked cuddled on the couch.

*Just like when we were kids,* she thought.

******

Meanwhile, City was having a holiday celebration early. Santa Claus came to town, and boy did he receive a present!

You see, being that Escalade put a hurtin' on Spruce Street business, City thought he'd come out a little earlier than usual to make up for the previous day's disaster. However, Spruce Street is a heroin block from 6 A.M. to 1 P.M. The Feds had it under surveillance, and just so happened to be conducting a reverse sting.

City surveyed the area, riding slow with his foot on the brake. Noticing a lot of new faces and none of the regular dope dealers, he tried to keep it moving.

Unfortunately, his name and description was one of the first the other dealers had given up to save their own asses. The main focus was to arrest the people from the suburbs, confiscate their vehicles, and fine them heavily for revenue purposes. Then again, City was a pretty big fish and prime candidate for a three-time loser.

It all happened so quickly. The other end of Spruce Street was blocked off by a U-Haul truck, with heavy firepower pointing in City's direction. Santa Clause revealed that he had plenty of elves and sleds!

With everything happening so fast, City's worker jumped out of the car with about nine ounces of powder in his hand, trying to make a dash. In a matter of seconds, you would have thought someone sang, "Let it snow, let it snow, let it snow!" All you could see was white powder flying everywhere.

The ten rounds of rapid gunfire put City's worker, Bone, to

rest immediately.

"Sponge Bob Wet Pants" struck again, because piss escaped City for the second time, and he was beyond shook; he was "shizook!" with trembling hands hanging clearly out of his car window. He waited for the Feds to extricate him from the vehicle.

You could see people peeking out of their windows. City was definitely on his own. Getting slammed headfirst and cuffed, the agents searched him quickly for weapons and led him to a black Lincoln with tints. He was whisked off immediately.

At the scene, it was radioed in that nothing else was found in the car. However, City's worker, Bone, had a firearm on him, and since the gun and drugs were in City's car, he could be charged with possession and conspiracy to sell narcotics—a third and final strike.

Overhearing the radio transmission, City was ready to " Let's Make a Deal!" Before even getting to the bureau, City agreed to do whatever it takes wear a wire, snitch about drug deals, and murders.

******

Fred turned a couple of corners, waiting for D.B. to call. He kept his eyes open for City and his crew, not knowing that City was tied up at the moment. He kind of wished D.B. had some of his heat holders available today just in case.

*It wouldn't hurt to mention it as soon as he calls,* he thought.

Stopping at the two/four, Fred strolled in. His jewels were gleaming like he hadn't a care in the world. His confidence was at an all-time high. By just looking at him, you could tell he was a boss. All of a sudden, he felt safe because although this store never closed, it was miles away from the hood. They don't bootleg, sell quarter waters or loosies. Therefore, 7-11 isn't a true two/four.

Finally D.B. called. "Escalade, what's goodie?"

"You already know. Waiting on you."

"Okay, okay," D.B. said.

Fred smoothly added, "Do you think your men can be around today just in case something pops off?"

"Give me like an hour," D.B. responded. "I'll make a call. They right in Philly. What's that, not even forty-five minutes away?"

Relieved, Fred said, "I'm about to get a quick chop. Just holla when they touch down. Who knows? You might be able to put your mans on your team and I have you regulate them. I've seen your work. I can fuck with Idaho, but Philly niggas! They hard, but grimy than a motherfucka. It's peace, though, 'cause 'that's your mans'," he said, laughing because he bit a line from the movie, *Belly*.

******

D.B. couldn't believe how easy it was to blow up in the game. In just one day, he'd already been able to bring in some of his crew, by request.

"Hello, Doug, you there?"

"Yes, good morning. How did you know it was me?" D.B. asked.

"Caller ID, Doug," Stan said.

"Oh, you got to get with the program. My hood name is D.B., and I'm straight out of Idaho. Are the twins around?"

"Yeah. What you up to?"

"Nothing. Just need a new jack crew to help me run things. Tell them we're going *hood*."

"Okay, will do. Be safe," Stan reminded him.

Doug sped on the parkway in his all black Acura with limo tint and New York plates. By the time he arrived, the twins were waiting outside, ready to go. They jumped in and Doug was in motion.

He informed them of the drama with City and how it came to gunplay. The twins smiled, indicating they loved drama.

After a quick stop to pick up bigger heat and an extra vest for Escalade, Doug's persona went back to D.B. mode and the twins would simply be known as "One" and "Two" from Philly. They all agreed.

******

47

"Yo, Escalade, everything is good. Meet us at the spot in fifteen minutes. When niggas act cold, we got heat!" D.B. said, hanging up the phone.

Escalade was relieved and excited because now he had power. As soon as he pulled up, everyone jumped in and D.B. turned down the music for a brief introduction. After seeing one of the twins with a book bag, Fred's thoughts had certainty.

Breaking the silence as they merged onto the highway, Fred announced that he was taking his new crew to lunch. What better way to gain loyalty than breaking bread?

To his surprise, D.B. spoke of a gift the twins brought with them, and handed over a brand-new black Kevlar vest. It was the newest on the market and went unnoticed beneath a button-up.

Fred really felt gangsta now, and once inside the restaurant, he insisted everyone eat whatever and how much they wanted. It sounded good, as if Escalade was ballin'. Then once they saw the Chinese man and smelled crab legs and fried chicken, they knew it was a buffet.

There wasn't much small talk as they ate. Everyone let Escalade lead the way. D.B. just assured him that One and Two knew how to handle whatever, and clap like an audience.

Getting back in the truck to head for the block, Two lifted up his throwback Sixers jersey (number 6, of course), causing Escalade to stare in amazement at, not one, but two Mac Eleven's he had concealed all the while.

Escalade was now ready for whatever. Drifting in his own thoughts, Texas 06 roared through the system: "Try'na catch me ridin' dirty…" as he crowned himself the new king. He had a crew now, and D.B., One, and Two kept it gangsta – a true example of bad boys moving in silence.

Posting up on the block, D.B. got it poppin'. Some people saved the money D.B. took from City to cop with today. Many were really happy and embraced D.B. like he was a lifelong friend or hero.

One and Two just observed things, watching out for anything suspicious. They were amazed at how D.B. had such a warm welcome in the hood already.

Escalade was on his phone acting like the busiest man in the world. It looked good, but deep down, he still felt nervous because City still posed a threat.

The evening went on without incident, especially since Escalade received a call that the Feds rushed Spruce Street and killed Bones and bagged City. However, City would probably put up a house and bond out eventually, because it's always more practical to fight a case from the street.

Money was coming, and Escalade bought soda and pizza for the entire block. He admired how none of the crew drank liquor or smoked weed while posted up.

One was like, "Staying on point is the first step to survival out here in this paper chase."

Two added, "Ya get in and out because it's not a game; shit is real!"

After selling out again, they headed back to the spot. There, One went to get the Acura that D.B. picked them up in, and noticed it had a New York plate. He pushed a button, the plate began to scroll, and he stopped it on the Pennsylvania marker.

Escalade was pleased with today's success, and insisted everyone get up tomorrow and discuss this paper. They all agreed, and before departing, playing big-time, Escalade broke off $1,500 for their pockets to show love and power, sealing a deal yet to be made.

# Chapter Nine

## Back to Work

Another day, another dollar, it seemed, judging by the snail pace all of the correctional officers. A ten-minute briefing about gang tension and a possible lockdown was evident.

Jazz and Mia punched in and went on their way, not even acknowledging Snow White. It was better that way, so no one expected their affiliation or association if shit ever hit the fan.

After the first tour, Jazz went on her way to handle business. She met with Snow White briefly, saying they'd meet at their usual spot, the public library, at one o'clock. Snow White and she would bring the kane, pass it off to Brianna and Akbar, and be paid within seventy-two hours.

Snow White's payment was more of dick and promises, plus a little cash; whereas Brianna and Jazz were about their dough. It worked out fine that Brianna was cool like that, and since having a cell phone, she handled a lot of money via wire transactions for the Gods. Some accounts were bogus, while some used government names of family members.

******

"How you doing, handsome?" Jazz asked, approaching Born Freedom.

"Real good now," he answered, playing with his hard dick.

"So, where are your neighbors? In court?" she asked, noticing both cells were empty to the right and left of him.

Born told her that they both work in the kitchen now and were getting dinner ready.

Seeing Born's dick poking out of his boxers, Jazz, being horny as hell, had an idea. She told Born she'd be right back. Trying to walk normally back to the bubble, she told Mia to keep a look out for about a half-hour, and she'd be right back.

Mia knew what time it was and kind of envied the sexual healing that was about to go down. Then again, she had her own plans.

Jazz eased the key into the lock and turned it slowly. Born was ready. Immediately, Jazz began sucking his dick off. Trying not to make slurping sounds, she licked balls and all while she pulled down her pants halfway. Her pussy was wet as hell, and you could smell the good pussy cookin' between her legs.

Born ran his fingers across her slit and began licking the juices from his strong fingers. Although they wanted to make love to one another, they knew there was only enough time to fuck.

Born begged, "Just let me lick that pussy from the back."

Not waiting for an answer, he licked her pussy doggy-style and stuck his tongue dead in her tight asshole.

Jail must bring out the freak in niggas for real, because as soon as that tongue hit that asshole, Jazz was nuttin' like a motherfucker. She reached back and aimed that dick dead in her soakin' wet sugar bowl.

Born worked that pussy like a rapist, too serious to miss a beat. The sounds of fucking were in the air, and Jazz gave a fuck less about a job. His balls were smacking that ass hard, and then the freak slipped out of her.

"Born, cum in my ass, nigga! Put that big-ass dick in my tight ass! Make me love you, nigga! Yeah, stick it all the way in!"

51

They were definitely in the zone. As his body began to tense, sweat pouring, and Jazz not giving a fuck, she let out a scream of her own as she felt his hot coffee fill her cup.

Trying to get it together, she dressed quickly and toweled her face dry from all the sweat. She splashed a few dabs of Muslim oil (Blue Nile) on her and headed back to the bubble.

Born had to call her back because the dick must've been so good, she left his cell wide open.

She laughed and said, "You're free, baby!" and headed back, only to realize she never asked him how much to bring tomorrow. Before she left, though, she'd find out.

Mia swore up and down that she heard them fucking, and Jazz looked like she had just got done either fuckin' or break dancing.

"I'm glad you're back because I gotta piss," Mia greeted.

Without a response, she headed to her spot next to Brianna's cell to piss and get a quick one in, because she was a little hot and bothered, knowing that the "brick shit-house" had been just a few feet away fucking Jazz like crazy.

Brianna doesn't miss a beat and played sleep to eavesdrop on the sound of her piss hitting the water. It was a good stream, and the "Brian" in Brianna was getting hard. Now, not normally being turned on by a woman, he had to admit and realize he was a lesbian, too, having served a year already.

Mia, thinking Brianna was asleep, sat there and began to play with her pussy, letting out soft moans, but her bracelets made a steady rattle. Brianna and she were at a rhythmic pace. It had been quite a while for both of them, and since they were both masturbating secretly, it wouldn't take long for an explosion.

Both speeds increased. Mia humped her three fingers, and Brianna was beating his dick as if the man came out for this nut. Mia must have blew a valve because steam was coming from that pussy when she came, causing Brian to remember the times and Lil' Jon, too, "Ah, skeet, skeet, skeet!"

Mia got herself together and "woke" Brianna up.

"Hey, girl!" she said.

Brianna acted like she just woke up, but had a little perspiration on her face, as well.

"You got some perfume for me? I need to freshen up a bit."

"And what were you doing to be so fishy?" teased Brianna, causing Mia to blush and wonder if Brianna heard her fingering her pussy. "Anyways, I got you, sister-girl, but next time, just let a bitch watch!"

"Oh, yeah! You got me good with that 'queen' shit. I thought you meant Latin Queen because you are fine as hell. I would have never known. So did you hear me?"

Laughing, revealing a beautiful smile, she said, "Hear you what?" Brianna acted innocent. "By the way, you seem cool as hell. I got a question. You know a girl be making moves in here, okay?"

Acting, Mia missed the point, because her response was in reference to sexual intercourse with other men, which according to the rules was prohibited.

Brianna laughed and left it alone, assuming she must not know anything. After all, she was new and just a couple of days on the job.

In a way, that was a relief because Brianna kind of liked her in a "Brian" way. She then asked Mia if she knew the warden's evil-ass.

Mia wondered why she referred to him as evil, but once Brianna told of how Warden Brown's son, Mike, and he went to boarding school and shared rooms and secrets for four years, she'd get the picture.

"Mike used to have nightmares all the time. I thought it was because he lost his mother in a car crash, but it was worse. His father used to rape him and force him to have oral sex with him. The warden is happier than a faggot with a bag of dicks, and as crooked as they come. What better place for him to work than here? He'll have his day…watch!" Brianna, teary-eyed, promised.

With all that said, Mia had to make it back to the bubble before Jazz got to worrying, and so she could also put her up on the gossip.

****** 

Snow White had mentioned to Akbar that tomorrow's move wouldn't be a problem; everyone was all set on the details. She also told him that she would have some extra money soon from her parents' real estate deal. Just knowing his greed, he banged her harder from the back, as expected. One thing she didn't need was money. To her, Akbar had the best dick around, and that's what mattered. She'd do anything to maintain her position in his life. She even wondered if it was a fatal attraction just waiting to happen, because once he was out and tried to leave her, he'd be swimming with the fishes, she swore to herself.

****** 

At about midnight, Snow White sat on her sofa, sipping a glass of wine, trying to unwind. She enjoyed the view of her saltwater fish aquarium, while dressed in her panties and listening to some slow jams. Feeling the peaceful effects of the entire scenery, Mia was heavy on her mind. Following the arousal of her moistening lower lips, she decided to call.

Amazed to hear her phone ring, lying in bed stroking her clit, Mia answered. "Hello."

"Mia, this is Snow from work. You busy?"

"No, not really, just lying in my bed," Mia said.

"Oh, you're in your night clothes already?" Snow White wondered for real.

"If you call a bedspread clothes, because I always sleep naked."

"Wow! That's very interesting. I bet... I mean..." Uncomfortably, Snow stammered.

Mia heard her and had to admit to herself that the voice on the phone had her wetter than ever, and she wanted to go there.

"Interesting how? Because I'm curious to know what you have on right now, since you know I'm naked, sexy."

"Oh, I'm glad you asked," said Snow White. "I'm on my leather sofa finishing my second glass of wine, taking off these wet-ass panties so I can fuck myself while thinking of you."

"I see you're not shy," Mia whispered.

By now, they both knew it was too late to turn back.

Snow White, being the aggressor, took charge. "Mia, does it feel good, baby? I know that pussy is wet. Yeah, open your legs wider. Make me eat it good. Don't be shy. I'ma make it feel real good. Pull my long, blonde hair. Yeah, like that. Work them hips, too. I want to taste your hot chocolate. Just imaging me licking you all over, and I do mean *all over*. You know I want you bad. You don't have to do nothing but be there, and I'll do the rest. Rub your pussy faster, baby, and squeeze those brown tits for me. Let me lick those black-ass nipples. You ready, baby? You ready? Oh shit! Here it comes, Mia! Fuck, Mia, here it comes! Oh, I'm cum'in!"

Mia moaned and shocked herself. "Oh, Snow White! I'm cum'in, bitch! I'm cum'in, bitch! You cum'in for me, too, bitch? Yeah! Yeah! Make me eat your shaved pussy, too! I wanna taste you, too. Oh, I'm cum'in!"

There was silence for a few minutes, and then Mia said, "Well, first time for everything, and I guess this is our first little secret. See you tomorrow, sexy. Good night!"

Snow White said goodnight, then reached between her legs for one more round before falling asleep.

# Chapter Ten

### Breaking the Cipher

After rec, Born Freedom and Malik were able to hook up. Born used his juice card and was allowed recreation with the dorm. There wasn't much movement due to some sort of tension caused by the Feds shooting a Black man in a drug bust. However, that was an in-the-world issue, and hype caused by the media. Inside the bing was their world for at least the next two calendars.

"Born, on my word, Akbar ain't right. I realize he's been down for a decade and has changed, but how is he going to dance with the devil? He taught me and you, 'The devil this...The devil that...'," Malik said, while spitting on the ground to emphasize his disgust.

"True, true. It seems as though the money has become our foundation, not our lessons. Just because Akbar has Snow White making moves, she's not the only C.O. 'bout it. He knows that bitch poison! Yo, she do got a big butt and a nice smile, though," Born said, as if almost understanding Akbar's situation.

"Fuck that! Me and you gon' turn this shit around and make it right for the rest of the Cipher. No one person or profit is beyond getting dealt with. After all the work we've put in, choppin' the heads off snakes is righteous!"

Malik's sword was his word, and Born Freedom knew there were about to be some serious changes.

This being an opportune time, Born mentioned the new deal he could and already planned to execute with Ms. J. Malik liked the idea of a free kilo for thirty days. That was more than enough time to get ahead of the game.

Born thought, *We're going to have to get rid of Akbar and Snow White eventually, because once we step to him, that bitch might act up. You know how dick-crazy them devils get. That's why we don't suppose to sex them. They try to suck the God out of you. Word!*

"I got a $5,000 deposit on plastic right now for half a key this week. Remember my man, Larry who used to do me favors because I caught him with a punk that time?" Malik reminded.

"You mean Sissy Larry, the C.O.? Yeah, and that dude put me up on a lot of hot gossip, like a real bitch."

"Like what?" Born asked, inching closer.

"Shit, he said he didn't become a lieutenant last week because of his intellect. Quiet as it's kept, Larry said the warden been had sugar in his tank, and they had finally recognized one another from one of those swinger bullshits out in New York a couple of years back."

Born became excited. "That's what it is, 'cause, fam, I shagged Ms. J. crazy yesterday. I broke her in half and she about this dough. Even she was on some 'fuck that white bitch' shit. I can have her hit us tomorrow with the half. We slow roll the other shit from Akbar and start getting new links."

"Well, Larry can line up two mommy C.O.'s and get us more hanger money up in here that we be sleeping on. Larry is my man and I fuck with him but he be on that "I ain't touching shit unless it's already inside." Malik concluded.

"But peep the fly shit: I gotta get with Brianna to set up another account since we're about to do us and them. Feel me?

Then I'll see Ms. J. and handle that. Yo, you should try to hook up with her girl that just started here. She right!"

"I'm good," Malik interjected, thinking about the bus ride.

"And what's 'hanger money'? Some new shit you learnt when you were in the world'? Born asked.

"Naw, I just made that shit up," Malik laughed. "It's hanger money because for that yay, niggas be coming out the closet!"

******

Like clockwork, Jazz was in route to the library to meet Snow White. It would only take about fifteen minutes, but a half made it look better.

As she pulled in, she noticed Snow White's truck already there with no one inside, just as normal as could be. Dropping her book in the daytime return slot, she smiled to acknowledge the librarian's greeting and went browsing, keeping track of time.

At one o'clock, she entered the restroom to find Snow White already on point with the girdle ready. Jazz unzipped and removed her sweatsuit jacket, while Snow White helped her slip the girdle on. Jazz was almost certain that, Snow White purposely took extra time fumbling around her breasts for a cheap thrill.

Snow White removed the compressed slabs of yay and they quickly stuffed the front of the girdle and tightened it as they went along. In all of three minutes, Jazz had checked out a book and was headed home to get dressed for work. Snow White waited and browsed a bit more, grabbing an offshore banking book and a murder mystery.

******

When Born Freedom reached the tiers, he went to check on Akbar to make sure everything was a go for that night. Akbar was overconfident with his connect and lover, and assured Born everything was everything. Born knew deep down he wanted to spare Akbar and just have him shipped out, because he knew Malik didn't have a problem enforcing the rules.

"So, Akbar," Born began, "what's the deal with you and Snow White? It seems like you were supposed to get her open and have her making hella moves for us. Then again, you act like she's wifey. I respect you and all, and you've taught me a lot, just as well as the others. But it is what it is. What's really good?"

"How are you going to bring that to me after all I've done for all of you? I've made y'all niggas rich. Y'all had change on the streets, and now you're gonna go home with paper in your pockets. What, since your boy Malik back, you don't like the way things are going? I tell you what: I have seven more years, and at least she'll be doing them with me. And yeah, we fell in love!" Akbar finally confessed.

"Peace, God. It ain't that. Right now, you got me feeling some type of way. I don't know who you are anymore. You used to be Akbar, but now you're on some sentimental shit. Let's just get money and we'll talk."

Born said what he said, walking away without salutation.

Malik, in the meantime, was getting with Larry about their deal over a slice of bean pie that Larry brought in, recalling it to be Malik's favorite. Just on appearances, you'd never guess C.O. Larry was gay, and he insisted he was bi.

"So, L, who's the C.O. bitches you got for me, and what's up with this warden?" Malik questioned.

"Well, I fuck Leeza from time to time, and I met her cousin Becca before we hooked her up with a job right after you left. Now, they don't know I love meat and fish, so let's keep it that way. We all smoke trees together, drink, and take a 'toot' every now and then. Lately, though, those two bitches be having me rollin' on those E pills. Shit, they probably fuckin' each other, because they always dancing, hugging, and grinding on each other. Imagine when I'm not around!" Larry said, trying to picture his words.

"Now, as for the warden, do you really want the details, or just a little 411?" Larry asked.

"L, you got me fucked up already thinking about the mommies. When will I get to meet them bitches? And I need the details on the warden just in case we have to turn his sweet ass into one of us, ya heard?"

"No disrespect, because you know we don't work like that, but Warden Brown don't give a fuck about nothing but fucking. He's dominant and submissive. He stays high, and oh, he knows everything going on up in here…trust! Warden Brown has eyes and ears everywhere. Some of the hardest, righteous gangsta niggas be straight snitching. As a matter of fact, so many motherfuckas are doing it that it's considered 'cooperating'. He's not trying to stop it because he's either poking the nigga or the nigga be poking him on the low. Shit, you'd be surprised! In that little bit of time you were out – what was it, almost two years? – niggas play pro baseball! They pitch, catch, and I joined in for a double play once my damn self!" L rejoiced.

"Naw, Larry, you bullshittin'?" Malik hoped. "It's like Sodom and Gomorrah in this piece. The wardens know the God's getting money, too?" he questioned.

"Malik, I hate to burst your bubble, but one of your main 'people's' name steady ringing by the brass. Word is, though, the warden is saving his ass because they fucking. What happened was Snow White is suspect, and the white guards don't like her always up in niggas' faces. Plus, every time they try to pinch 'him', he's clean. What fucked me up was she tried to save his ass by fucking the warden so they wouldn't transfer the nigga when he tried to sell me and her out and end up getting fucked by the warden his damn self; I mean fucked in the *gay* way, too! The warden is a freak and records shit like that. One night, we watched it together before we got busy. I swear to God; and you know who I'm talking about!"

With all that, Malik had to smoke a cigarette. He never would have imagined shit was so fucked up. It was bad enough Akbar was fucking a devil, but the gay shit and the snitching! There was no room for error, and it was already settled once it became a proven fact by at least two believers. If only Malik could get the tape it would be justified.

Lt. Larry did look out and arrange for Born to check back with Malik at every evening rec before any further moves were made. He definitely didn't want Born caught up in all of the bullshit, with about only twenty-four months left.

## Chapter Eleven

### Boys Will Be Boys

City made the news and headlines after posting a half-million dollar bond. That was quite a chunk for him to be able to touch under such short notice. In the hood, that was impressive, and even Escalade had to rethink his assumptions of him.

Stan received a call from Roger. They were old college rivals who enjoyed irritating one another.

"Hey, Stan, hear about Spruce Street?" Roger asked.

"Couldn't miss it. The headlines were everywhere. Good job as far as taking drugs off the street, yet why another brother killed for nothing? The article said there was no weapon drawn and the gun was found still tucked in his waistband, concealed!"

"Stan, you still trying to justify and save your bros, I see."

"Hey, Roger, one fuckin' day you're gonna read a white male found dead, ruled a suicide due to multiple gunshot wounds to the back and cranium. Good day, buddy! You're such a good ole boy!" said Stan, hanging up the phone.

Roger laughed to himself, thinking the G-code ain't what it

used to be.

Escalade and his crew, D.B. and One and Two, were posted on the One Way and money was coming, as usual. The music was bumping and jump-offs were jumpin', while chicken-heads were gobblin'.

Escalade stayed horny and was always game to get a little concentration, but he had to take a rain check because there were too many witnesses. Being the boss and all, a twenty-dollar slappin' (dick suck) wouldn't appear gangsta to the crew, he figured. However, he had plans for them tonight…strip club!

Everything was straight until City's car was spotted coming down the One Way. He blew his horn to let D.B., especially, know he was approaching. One and Two were on point, guns drawn, ready to blaze. Escalade was trying not to jump out of his skin.

D.B. commanded, "Pull over, pussy and state your case!"

City got out, hands in the air, inviting someone to search him to show he came in peace. "Yo, I no come for no beef business and ray-ray. Me need to chat with da brotha, Escalade, sien?"

Relieved, Escalade just had to play gangsta. "What up, rude boy? You wan' work, 'cause me no da big rasclot bon done broke your foot a'ready!" he mocked, sounding Jamaican. "So, wop'n, Winston?" knowing a lot of Jamaicans with that name.

"Tru' t'ing, star. Me link not reach me and left me for dead. Me gwan brush 'em when the time come and even all of we become rich at one blood clot time. Me not want fa war, and be a deportee boy. Me just wan' fa flex and lash up some gal and everyt'ing, criss. Now, general, what ya half for me until me line up da jook? Spruce Street done an'a police boy cannot see me upon da road. Me set up shop in da Heights and big up t'ings for all of we bergin."

"Sounds good," Escalade said. "D.B., you hear this pussy clot?"

"Chill, boss. It sounds good because we make more money by covering more territory. Plus, we all have to eat anyway. It's too hot to be beefing with one another. If City plays it right and we get to rob his old connect, we all paid. Just like the Army, Navy,

Airforce, and Marines, they different with one common interest. *Ours*, of course, is to get MOB, money over bitches!" D.B. clarified.

"Alright, alright. Mr. Negotiator, it's on you," Escalade shifted the responsibility. "You talk to the nigga; you touch him with something later tonight, ya heard? As a matter of fact, let's all meet at eight, grab some dinner, and put it together. How about Hal's on Main Street, because I have a taste for steak and eggs, and they serve everything there.

Everyone agreed. D.B. and City were secretly relieved that everything remained peaceful this time around.

It was almost seven, so Escalade wanted to go grab some work to give D.B. for City and freshen up before dinner. He told the crew not to make plans because tonight they were ballin'!

One and Two liked the sound of that. After all, they were the youngest and loved to party.

They all met on time, and shared a large round table with about enough space for at least eight. The food was great, just as Escalade predicted, and you could tell everyone was full because no one said a word.

"Yo, D.B., you ride with City so you can pass off that work to him, and y'all discuss what type of business it is. City, you know where Teaser's at up the block on the left, right? Just meet us there. One and Two can follow me in their car. Okay, we're gonna need three cars, too, because we all fuckin' some bitches tonight."

With that, Escalade got them talking and anxious to go.

The parking lot indicated a nice crowd, which was typical for a Friday night. Once security saw Escalade pull up, they unhooked the chain and allowed him to park right up front in VIP parking. Almost anywhere he went people admired his truck and the way he threw money around.

Others noticed all three vehicles pulling up back-to-back and weren't sure if that was a sign of trouble. Many recognized City and wondered what type of mood he was in, and the all-black Acura made people feel some type of way.

Security embraced Escalade, but were surprised to see him

and City together, and nodded at the other three new faces, ushering them all into VIP.

The music was loud and clear. The lights were dead right. With Escalade leading his entourage headed by security, they definitely were turning the heads of dancers on stage and wanna-be hustlers and haters. With just head nods to acknowledge a few people, they were seated comfortably to awaiting big bottles. Escalade tipped security and the waitress for being on point with the bottles.

The tempo slowed down and April politely asked if they wanted any company. The twins were all smiles and not regular drinkers, so it only took two glasses for them to feel nice. After getting the okay from Escalade, security let April and two of her girls in VIP.

"Yes, bergin, dis is how we flex back in yard! We make da money and live like rasclot kings. See, me like your style a'ready. Toast to da general!" City saluted.

Hands were everywhere, and in VIP it wasn't a problem. More bottles were sent over, as well as more bitches. The dee-jay knew exactly what to play to keep the party going. She played "Shake What Ya Momma Gave You", "Drop It Like It's Hot" and "Money Ain't A Thang".

The ladies were enjoying VIP, and other patrons had to admire the way they were truly ballin'. However, April and her crew were professionals. They enjoyed the drinks, the 5's and 10's and 20's. However, to get into deep pockets, she knew there had to be some dick suckin' and fuckin'. That's why the last three bottles had plenty of E pills in them, and everyone was rollin' whether they knew it or not.

April said, "Escalade, this shit almost over. Can we all go to the Turnpike and really get it poppin'? You know how we get down. I'll go get my bitches ready and we'll meet y'all in the lot in fifteen. Cool, baby boy?"

Escalade was one year younger, and he enjoyed her calling him 'baby boy'. After getting with his crew out in the lot, it took a little convincing, with one slight interruption; a drunk-ass hater.

"Y'all niggas think y'all the shit!" said Stew, an up and coming nobody, feeling his liquor. "I should rob you motherfuckas!"

Stew's boys were making matters worse, but not realizing Two had two Mac Eleven's pointed at their entire clique. D.B prayed for nothing to go wrong, while Escalade tested City's loyalty already.

Once Stew and his crew saw City approaching, it was too late. One hitter quitter, Stew was out for the count. Stew's people emptied their pockets and took off their jewels without being told. City really had gorilla in him and wasn't letting anything stop tonight's fringe benefits of a true baller.

He turned and asked, "Yo, who wan a chain or lickle bling-bling for ya wrist or finga? Me not floss; me a top shotta, sien!"

One and Two eagerly accepted the jewels. D.B. knew they were acting strange. Even he, himself, couldn't stop grittin' his teeth and was thirsty as hell.

To show he was down, City handed Escalade a handful of money, without even counting it, which was donated thanks to Stew and company.

The women finally came out, and April told them to just get in and be nice, because they're all going to the same place. She noticed extra jewelry in the twin's hands and noticed someone laid out in the parking lot. That was a clear sign that some things never change. *Niggas!*

As the three vehicles pulled out, shots rang. Since Escalade and D.B. were in the first car and City was in the second car headed down the street, One pulled over and Two jumped out, dumping both clips into the parking lot, and then they drove off, catching up with their convoy.

Eventually, they'd realize that a bullet hit one of the guys in the head, killing him instantly.

D.B. thought he heard shots ring out, but the twins denied it. Being that they were all rollin', that subject was done with fast.

The entire entourage hit the turnpike and followed Escalade in front, City in the middle and the twins in the back all pulled into the Courtyard at Marriott on the Turnpike. I got out and got us a double suite.

The girls weren't prostitutes, so to speak, but expected to get paid or if they had to, rob these niggas. The guys were super horny, so payin a trick wasn't an issue.

They all coupled up and went to find their own private spaces. There were two bedrooms, a bathroom, a living room and kitchen – just enough space, but not enough condoms. On the low, a couple of them were about to "spin the wheel". Ain't no way that pussy was going to escape tonight, and of course, spinning the wheel is extra because of the risk factors involved.

April had D.B. naked in record time. Being Mr. Level-head went out the window. She had his toes curled up in no time. He was sweating and breathing like he had been chased. His drinks had a hold on him, too, because he came right inside her – raw – and went to sleep.

Escalade had China in the bedroom, trying to make love. He should've known the playa rules: when you're jumpin' off, you're not supposed to eat the pussy. The ecstasy had him Mr. Sensitive Holmes, 'cause he was begging to taste it. He licked toes, ass, and whatever else she stuck into his mouth. She fucked him to sleep, too. She was afraid to rob him, but he'd wake up one-thousand dollars short.

City had Big Wanda in the living room. They both needed space because they had too much energy. They sounded like he was talking Jamaican and she was talking African, humping like two motherfuckers mating on the Discovery Channel, gruntin' and sweatin', their bodies smacking like they were in a sumo-wrestling match. City must have been on the tiger bone, because they fucked until daylight. Stew's pinky ring he had kept was fair exchange.

The twins did just what Denise and Keisha figured. They kept switching all night, acting like it was just one of them fucking all that time. No one minded, but it would cost them, because those two bitches hated sore coochies in the morning. They came off with two platinum chains and iced-out medallions.

By checkout, the ladies had quietly left by cab, who knows exactly when. Each left numbers to be reached, which was polite for a hoe.

The fellas knew they had secrets, and some private discussions to partake in.

City was damn near in love with Big Wanda, and definitely planned on getting her to come out to the Heights and chill with him.

Escalade figured they'd hit the One Way about five or six o'clock because he was still tired.

D.B. thought that would give him time to replay what the hell went on last night. One thing D.B. realized was that April had some fire, oil, grease...whatever good pussy was called these days.

# Chapter Twelve

### It's Poppin'

Jazz and Mia were both riding dirty. While still wearing their Kevlar vests on top of their tightly-strapped girdles, their power move became undetectable. The vests were part of their daily dress code. However, the "bout it" C.O.'s normally declined to wear them as their personal option. After all, their crew enjoyed revealing cleavage.

Right after count, Jazz had Mia's delivery to Brianna concealed in a bedroll. "Yo, make sure she believes you don't have a clue as to what's going on," Jazz reminded Mia.

Mia headed out to execute her first power move in the bing, while Jazz had three p.m.'s to make. Walk and toss was all she had to do regarding Smitty and Tone. This was on a regular for them. Born knew the routine, as well, yet with two different packages, he'd try making small talk, hopefully leading up to a quickie.

As soon as she approached Born's cell, he had the stash spot on the TV, ready to cuff the work. The entire back snapped on and off, lined with coffee so the one K-9 at San Dora could never pick up the scent. He wondered how much she'd bring, because they never confirmed face to face an amount. It was just from a distance that he gave her hand signals as she was leaving to go home last night.

Jazz had figured since he signaled one half, he had to mean half a brick, because a half-ounce was no money to split. Secondly, when he tapped on the wall, which was made of steel, he must have meant hard, because the amount was already understood.

"Oh, I see you're on your 'A' game today. You knew exactly what I was talking about," Born said, adding, "I need round two, ma. What about you?"

"Give it a minute. I gotta let this pussy marinate. You smoked my boots last time. Plus, it's too much going on right now to be try'na get naked. I'm 'bout whatever – trust – but a bitch still gets nervous and I'm try'na be on point, and your sexy ass got me trippin'."

Brianna waited until Mia was back in the bubble before unraveling the bedroll. She always used the cell-cam to record exactly what was received so there'd be no confusion or discrepancies. It could have been paranoia or a complex due to sexuality. Nevertheless, everyone had their own reasons.

After last chow, Born Freedom had moves to make, and since it was evening classification tonight, plus incoming from court, no one had time to watch him. With his juice card, and Lt. Larry working, carting a TV to the dorm for Malik wasn't obvious at all. It seemed quite normal amongst friends.

"Peace, God!" Malik exclaimed, acting happy to see Born.

However, he was really thrilled to see the mission accomplished. Malik recognized his old TV and knew it was money in the bank.

After embracing one another, Malik gave Born the plastic, as they went to the end of the aisle.

"You first," Malik insisted.

"Well, right now, man, all I gotta do is go check with Brianna, get us an account set up, and take the five G's off the plastic, right? Oh, then I'm supposed to grab some shit from Akbar.

He kind of tight with me because I asked him about Snow White, already knowing the answer. Ak' try'na say because you back I'm questioning him when he was the one putting money in all our pockets!"

"He's dead, dead *dead*!" Malik fumed. "You ain't gonna believe this bullshit, and dem punks don't be lying! Peep the fly shit. Fucking that devil ain't shit! L. told me that Akbar's a punk and a snitch. He seen on tape that the warden and Akbar are butt-buddies! Plus, he told on Snow White about making moves, trying to save his own ass. The thing is, the warden don't give a fuck about the drugs as long as he running up in something. Remember, that's how Larry became lieutenant, because they know each other on some down-low shit when it was first poppin' off."

"Enough said, God. My stomach hurt with all this happy-feet shit. Niggas be trippin' straight up," Born disgustedly stated.

"He's dead for just fuckin' the devil, and didn't he confess to you that they're in love? How can God love the devil? 'Y' is why you suppose to love hell, right? And in his case, destroy in order to build. I might be able to get the tape or set it up so we can speed dub it to show and prove actual facts," said Malik.

That was the beginning of a plan. Hopefully, they'd rise above their emotions and handle the matter properly and without error. Although there's no "CSI" investigation on the deaths of prisoners, murder still could carry life if caught. Gladly, most of that shit is just TV.

Born caught up to Brianna just in time. She was headed back to classification for the laundry job Snow White hooked her up with. That way, she'd have movement and access to the entire population, which would be a plus for their operation.

"I was just coming to see you," Born said.

"Can a girl get a rain check until later?" Brianna teased, irritating Born purposely.

"On business!" Born confirmed flat out.

"Okay, Mr. God-body. I was just joking."

"Don't make me bust your ass," Born threatened.

Brianna mumbled, "I wish!"

"Seriously, though," Born said, handing Brianna the card, "take $5,000 off this and open me and Malik a D.L. account. We got moves to make. It's big dough in it for you if you 'bout it," bargained Born.

"Well, as soon as I come from classification, I'll get right on it. You can pick up the card tomorrow, and your new D.L. information. So you and this Malik guy are pretty close, I see. Ain't nothing more refreshing than brothers on the down-low," Brianna joked, while laughing and running out of Born's reach.

******

The classification board consisted of three officers and the warden when the job consisted of movement throughout the entire facility.

The first screening would be done based on behavior and amount of sentence. Lastly, the warden would interview, alone in his office. If you were lucky, he'd get to you in about a week, but if he had the hots for you, he'd make time immediately.

Warden Brown heard about Brianna through the grapevine. He knew of her role laundering money and moving drugs in his facility. He also noticed her beauty while touring the housing units, and couldn't wait for the opportunity to present itself. Brown figured with a little finesse, and being that he had been looking the other way, he'd soon have his way with her, also.

Brian entered the warden's office with a useless attempt to appear masculine. Brianna was drop-dead gorgeous, with breasts and a nice ass. Trying not to drool, the warden introduced himself, failing to realize they once knew each other. After all those years and new temp-hormone shots later, there actually was no resemblance. Brianna's skin crawled after their handshake as she sat, intimidated by the old tales of abuse Mike Brown once narrated.

"So, what do you think?" Warden Brown asked, referring to his rather lavish office. "Care for a drink, cigarette, or toot, Brianna?" he asked, rubbing his nose.

"A drink would be nice, and a cigarette," she answered,

shocked that the warden knew her girlie name.

"My desk is a mess. Come on, let's sit over here and go over your file," he said, sitting on the sofa and opening a folder. "Looks like it's your first time in the 'big house', and I'm sure your last. You know you could have it made here and do sweet time if you act right. I tell you what. Your file indicates you've had some college, and it appears a B.A. in business. I just so happen to need help in here. It would be a shame to waste your time and intelligence doing laundry. And you still could roam the jail with *better* benefits!"

"I don't have benefits now, Mr. Brown," Brianna lied.

"Having a cell phone, making over a thousand dollars a week selling drugs, stashing drugs and makeup in your cell – I'd think you'd consider those benefits, since I've been looking the other way for quite some time!" Laying the cards on the table, so to speak, he added, "What do you think, I really don't know what's going on in my prison? I have sources, some you'd dare to believe. After being down for a while, a weak man's mind begins to play tricks on him. The slightest breeze gets a nigga's dick hard." Filling his jaws with air, he blew out. "See?" he added, grabbing his dick through his pants.

"Well, hold that thought and bone you'd like to pick. I'll see you in the morning, say nine-ish," Brianna concluded, narrowly escaping his clutches for the evening.

Buzzing a little from the drink, Brianna dipped down the hall, hoping to run into Born.

He was in his normal spot, playing sloppy seconds by the visiting room. Just by the rapid hand motion, Born could tell something was important and urgently needed his attention.

"Did you get the little jobby-job?" Born asked.

"Not the laundry job, but how about one better? As a matter of fact, make it simply unbelievable. After I tell you this shit, it's gonna be a wrap. Did you see Wanda Sykes when she was on "Jay Leno" in January 2007, when she said, 'Kill-a-hooker-money'?"

"What the hell is that?" Born asked, not familiar with what he thought was gay-gay talk.

"'Kill-a-hooker-money' is having California celebrity money – so much dough you can kill a hooker – or wife, like O.J. – and get away with it," Brianna explained.

"If you didn't get the laundry job, then how will we be able to make more money, especially this Kill-Bill money or whatever money?"

"I just left Classifications and was granted the second phase tonight, which is when the warden interviews you, as well. How y'all say it? 'Peep the fly shit.' The warden is with all the bullshit, and I do mean *all*! He knows about the drugs, money, my cell phone and makeup from the street. He said we'd be surprised as to who his sources are and how many hardcore niggas are on the down-low. That motherfucka is freaky, and it seems like he's doing him, and like things just the way they are. Now I know I'm sexy, but you haven't and ain't gonna hear about me fuckin' or suckin' shit. I got a man waiting on me, and I got my own dough before and after this shit. The warden hired me to be his office aide, so I have to see what's what. Already, though, he gonna grab at his shit, try'na show me it gets hard with the wind. He just don't know. I'll beat the brakes off his old freaky black ass…trust!"

"I believe you on everything you said because I just heard the same shit today from Malik in the dorm. We're going to have to keep this shit between us and act as normal as possible until we figure the safest way out. Heads are gonna roll, and although this place is full of them, we ain't taking no prisoners."

Brianna was down with the money making part, but Born sounded like he was about to push it to the limit. Profit is good, yet ain't no coming back from murder.

******

"La-La-La-Larry!" Singing that old rap song, Malik approached Lt. Larry happy as can be. This was a sure sign that it was all good. The lieutenant confirmed the remainder of the cost would be in the following day, plus he'd bring in a few pies for the brothers.

"Yo, L, when can I meet the mommies? You gassed me up,

and then left me on high hopes. With all this other next shit going on, I got moves to make, feel me?"

"I'm going to have them work tomorrow over here in the dorms. Usually, I have them third shift outside riding around the perimeter or doing hospital security, or tricking up in the towers somewhere. You know, I lay my pimp down!" Larry said, shaking his pinky ring and causing a good laugh. "Cool?"

"No doubt, that's straight."

# Chapter Thirteen

## Between Me and You

"Hey, Jazz, dis China. What up, hoe?"

"Oh, hey, slut. About time you called somebody back. I know you saw me and my girl, Mia, leaving tonight when you were coming in…late, as usual."

"I heard a horn blow, but I was still tired from the other night."

"The other night? What you done did now? Or should I say, who you done 'done' now?" Jazz asked.

"Girl, we worked the club five deep the other night. It was me, April, the damn ringleader, Big Wanda, Keisha, and Denise's trifling asses. We were getting our paper, as usual. Then some ballers came through. We got on some big bottles and lap dances up in the VIP, and April fucked around and put mad ecstasy in the second or third round, and had everybody rollin'. These niggas didn't know what hit 'em. We jumped off and definitely were ahead of the game by morning," China told her.

"Why you didn't call me for that good shit?"

"Jazz, I didn't know you still sell pussy. I thought you were just hustlin' a little in the bing."

"Shit, sellin' pussy *is* a hustle...the first and last. I just don't strip in the club no more. I told you, my friend, who's like my sister, her brother almost saw me one night. After that, it wasn't me no more. A woman does anything to get hers; she's quick to be a bitch or a hoe. Feel me? This pussy is always for sale, or you can rent-to-own!"

"You ain't know? We dem 'bout it' C.O. bitches. Treat a nigga like a pair of panties. In jail or out, for the right price they can get a little wet, too."

"So, China, you never said who the ballers were. Were they rappers or executive-type niggas just out trickin'?"

"One was a local I seen around, and maybe the other one, too. But the other three were definitely some Philly or New York niggas. Just before we were leaving the club to go jump-off, they laid one nigga out, and I swore somebody was bussin' shots, too."

"Girl, I know you bitches were ready to go when you heard shots ringing," Jazz said.

"Hell yeah! I was so tempted to pull my shit out and get it cookin'. You know we stay S.N.S.—sexy and strapped! Real talk, what fucked me up was I had to hop over the VIP velvet rope with heels to try and get in his truck. I reached to open the door and it had no handles. Then the shit don't open normal. This shit is tough. The nigga's doors is money, because those motherfuckas did cartwheels, sitting on some Crayola chromes. He *was* that video! Fuck try'na be!"

Jazz knew exactly who China had fucked: her lifelong secret love and best friend's brother, Fred AKA Escalade.

"Damn, China! You were ballin' then. Can that nigga fuck?"

"Can he?! That nigga work in the mailroom, 'cause when it comes to stamps and envelopes, he definitely was huffin' and puffin', lickin' and stuffin'!"

"How much you get out of him?"

"Two nuts, and I clipped him for a G, dat's all," China replied.

"Wow! You were being nice. You normally take it all."

"Naw, not him. Like I said, I've seen him around before. I think with the weave, contacts, and fashion tattoos he didn't recognize me."

"Oh, that's true. Plus, once a nigga gets tipsy and thinking with his dick, he ain't try'na recognize nothing but some wet pussy anyway."

"I gave him my number just in case he needs some more of 'all of this'! He's cute, too, and counting big dough. Shit, he needs to call!"

"Well, you're at work and I just got off. Thank you for making sure I knew I missed a good session, and the next time I'm getting fucked like crazy, I'll make sure *not* to call you, too, bitch! I'm 'bout to shower and lay it down. Holla!"

"Alright, Jazz, holla!"

That was all she needed to hear. Deep down, Jazz began to realize she had a real secret thing for Fred, and she felt some type of way hearing he fucked and sucked China. And did a good job at that! It had to be him, she thought. Who else had a truck like that around town but him? In the shower, she let her mind run wild, imagining what it would be like when she gave Fred some pussy!

******

"Hello, Mia. You still up?"

"Oh, hi, Snow. I see you're up. I just got finished nibbling on a Hot Pocket. What are you up to at these wee hours?"

"Well, I couldn't really sleep this early. I was thinking perhaps you'd like to come over for a glass of wine. We could watch a movie on my flat screen and even view it from the Jacuzzi. That is, of course, if you don't mind keeping me company. It wouldn't be a problem picking you up. I already have on a pair of sweats."

"Okay, that sounds good because I'm bored and wide awake. You know how to get here?"

"I'm five minutes away. Ciao!"

"Ciao!'

Already Mia was soaked just thinking about such a romantic setting of she and Snow finally naked in the Jacuzzi. She had only five minutes to put on fresh panties and try to dry her excitement before her ride arrived. In a flash, she was headed out the door.

The ride was quick and quiet. Once reaching their destination, Mia noticed Snow lived in a very nice upscale neighborhood.

"Please, make yourself at home," Snow said, as she unzipped her sweat jacket, revealing bare tits. "I hope you don't mind, because I was about to get in the tub before I ran out."

"No problem. I only have a bra on under my jacket," Mia laughed. "Might as well let the titties breathe. Anyways, we'll be in the water shortly and won't have on nothing but birthday suits and nail polish."

While Snow poured the wine, Mia couldn't help staring at her huge, white breasts. They were perfect, and her nipples poked holes in the air as they bounced.

Unnoticed, Snow slipped an ecstasy pill into Mia's drink to make certain she scored. Little did she know, Mia was more than willing to end her curiosities tonight. Be it ecstasy, wine, or lust, it was going down!

Snow placed the glasses on the side of the Jacuzzi, letting that be Mia's cue to come over. They decided on a porn movie – girl-on-girl, of course – because after their first phone episode, it wasn't hard to tell what would be next.

The Ecstasy pill didn't have a taste of its own, and the wine was a perfect blend. Heated perfumed water sensually soothed their now naked bodies. Enjoying the feel, they sipped their drinks, watching the screen to establish their mood.

Playing footsie and just letting the movie work its magic was the smoothest route to travel since it would be Mia's first time. Snow White loved the shine of her wet brown skin. The warm water meeting the room air caused Mia's chocolate nipples to beg for attention. Snow figured the ecstasy would be kicking in, plus, the wine and movie. Sliding closer, she made the first move.

"Wow! Your nipples are at attention just like mine. See?" she said, pointing at her own nipples. "Feel how hard mine are. Pinch them; that sends a charge straight to my cunt. Do you mind?"

Snow reached for Mia's left breast, cupping it in her hands. She began sucking and tonguing the nipple, causing Mia's eyes to close as she began to moan. With her free hand, she reached for Mia's pussy, which automatically leaped into her grip for fondling. Mia was hot and rolling, a perfect combination.

Snow slipped a finger inside of Mia just about an inch to tease her now jerking body. Directing every move, she led her to the bed, dripping wet and not knowing everything was being recorded.

Mia laid back while Snow began licking her all over, and once she reached that soaking pussy, Mia released her first climax physically caused by a woman. Snow continued licking Mia's pussy and forcefully ramming her middle finger in her asshole, causing her to cum like never before, screaming, "Oh shit, Snow! Fuck that ass, bitch! Fuck it good! Oh, I'm cum'in all in your mouth. Eat my pussy, bitch! Eat it!"

Without a hint, Snow spun around and was on Mia's face in a 69 position. Mia repeated what she felt being done to her. Her virgin tongue worked well. Mia licked her pussy, tasting those juices for the first time, loving it! Snow was grinding on her face, and they were both about to explode.

Snow screamed, "Yes, Mia! Yes, yes! Stick your finger in my ass. Harder, baby…*harder*! I'm 'bout to nut, baby. Cum with me! Cum with me! Ooooh, here it comes! I'm cum'in!"

Mia, without notice, began eating her asshole out, causing Snow to drench her face even more.

Mia blurted out, "I gotta piss, Snow!"

Snow jumped up and led her to the ledge of the Jacuzzi. Snow sat down on the side with her legs and feet in the water, and she directed Mia to face her and stand over her, straddling her body with her pussy inches from her face. Snow began rubbing her clit fast and rough and licking Mia's still soaked pussy.

Mia was enjoying it, but still had to piss.

Snow was squeezing Mia's ass cheeks, massaging really

rough, and demanded her, "Piss now!"

Snow White was a freaky bitch. Mia pissed in her face, watching it run down her breasts, stomach, and by the time it flowed directly to her clit, Snow was fucking four fingers by now and cum'in again.

Rinsing in the tub, they toweled off and laid in front of the fireplace on top of the black bearskin rug, just holding on to each other, kissing gently, and falling asleep with another secret.

******

Brianna arrived at the warden's office at 9 a.m. sharp, wondering what to expect. For starters, he instructed her to file sentence data forms in the pile of folders he left out, and he'd be back at about eleven. Perhaps then they could do lunch.

"Anything in particular you'd like for lunch? I was thinking Chinese, since they deliver," he asked.

"That's fine with me. Is it alright if I smoke in here while you're gone? I won't burn it down!"

"You can do whatever you want, sexy," the warden replied, biting his bottom lip in anticipation.

Brianna just looked around, not touching anything, because cameras were probably everywhere. To demonstrate good work ethics, by the time Warden Brown returned, the files he left her to do were complete.

"Wow! You're finished already? I need a drink and a toot!"

Pulling a mirror out of his desk drawer with lines already arranged, he sniffed one line, then two. He handed the mirror to Brianna, insisting just a little, while also pointing to the drink.

Not wanting to look suspect, Brianna took a couple of small toots and chased it with the Henny. However, the cameras were rollin', and that wasn't plain Henny either. Oh, it wasn't an E pill either. This was a knock-out drug Warden Brown learned to make while overseas in the military. Soon he'd have his way…rape!

Thinking it was the coke and Henny, Brianna sat down on the sofa, overly relaxed, already beginning to doze. The warden began gripping himself, sneaking a few feels on Brianna's tits to see if the drug was in full effect. Without any resistance, once again the warden became a predator.

Making sure the door was locked and the film rolling, Brown greased himself thoroughly with the KY Jelly, and with the other hand, began to undress and position Brianna on the sofa for rear penetration. This was his sick turn-on that meant more to him than a job, the law, and especially his nagging wife of thirty years.

Being in total control was the reason why he didn't mind turning the other way when things went on that was not supposed to. He had his choice and last word. Being the warden, he thought he was God because he could let you live or have you killed.

With so much anticipation, the dirty deed didn't last long, but to him it served its purpose. He dressed Brianna, washed the grease off his hands, and ordered lunch.

When Brianna finally woke up, she felt a burning sensation in her rear, but couldn't figure out why. Warden Brown assured her that she fell asleep and must not be getting enough rest.

The food arrived, and as they ate, there was no conversation. The stinging kept bothering Brianna, and she wondered what the hell happened, then doubted anything crazy because who wouldn't know something like that?

"I'm about to go lay down because I'm still feeling the drink, okay? I'll be in tomorrow at nine because I know you want me to get my beauty rest," she teased phonily.

The warden was hard already, sitting behind his desk, waiting to jerk off as soon as he was alone.

Brianna headed to the tier, feeling some type of way with every step, though. Once inside her cell, she reached down, noticing some sort of stain on her panties. Touching her asshole, trying to soothe the soreness, her fingers came up greasy, like a Slip-n-Slide.

An instant surge of violation overwhelmed her/him. Brian surfaced and Brianna cried, realizing what must have happened. Warden Brown did what he'd soon regret.

Thinking out loud and pacing hysterically, "No one will ever know, and he won't live to tell a soul. I don't give a fuck! I'ma kill that motherfucka dead! I can't go out like this. He raped me! But how? It must have been something in the drink, I bet! I'm too tall to hang myself in this little-ass cell. I have to think. I can't even call nobody on this shit. I just have to think!"

# Chapter Fourteen

**Breaking News**

The morning came and went like no other to everyone, because on every channel appeared the words:

"Breaking News: Shots rang out at approximately 2:30 a.m. at Teasers, a local strip club lately known for attracting johns, drugs, and now murder. A fatal gunshot to the head left one black male, in his mid-twenties, dead at the scene. Police have both an eyewitness and a suspect, and vehicle of significant interest. According to the witness, the shooter's vehicle was bulletproof. Yes, bulletproof! During an exchange of gunfire, bullets apparently bounced off the, what is to be believed, armored sports car.

"The victim's name is being withheld until the next of kin is notified.

"If you've seen this person," a sketch was shown on the screen, "or know the whereabouts, do not attempt to approach him because he's definitely believed to still be armed and dangerous. Call your local police. There is a reward for any information leading to his arrest and conviction.

"The police are on the lookout for a black Acura, with New York license plates and dark, tinted windows.

"This has been Shekeem Harold reporting for Channel 7, Hood News."

That news story had the bing buzzing with gossip and speculation. Some wondered if they knew who got shot, because of the locals appearing in the background on the news. Others were more fascinated by the bulletproof car. The possible suspect's picture shown was one nobody recognized. Therefore, the assumption was right; it had to be New York boys or someone from not around there.

"Yo, God, that was some G-Unit shit, getting it cookin' with bulletproof whips – fuck a vest! Now that's some futuristic shit," Smitty said.

"I told you, my dude, that's the type of shit me and my mans be on," said Old School. "Me and Malik be making hella moves out in the world. They caught us now on some new bullshit violation of probation for just coming into contact with the police, but they the ones came at us sideways."

"What Malik are you talking about? Not God-body Malik; brown skin, cock-diesel with dreads, right?" Smitty asked.

"Yeah, Get-Money-Malik," Old School replied.

"His crew is the Gods who got this joint on smash. You say you went down with him and he's here?" Smitty inquired.

"He's been in the dorm. His people know. Ask Born. Then again, I ain't try'na get you fucked up, feel me?" Old School capitalized on the moment, using what was said to his advantage. "Hey, Smitty, let me get a cup of coffee and a couple of soups 'til they send me a package from the dorm. Me and my mans trying to be on the low. You know how niggas be talkin'."

Smitty was impressed with all the bullshit Old School was kickin' and hooked him up with a crazy care package: socks, T-shirts, drawers, cosmetics, and mad food. Game recognized game, and Smitty wanted in on the big leagues once and for all. By putting Old School under the wing, he'd one day use that as an 'in', he thought.

Meanwhile, Jazz saw the breaking news and was trying to call Mia. After talking to China, she knew something wasn't right. However, Mia never picked up the phone and was probably either in the shower or asleep.

Hot gossip didn't stop there. Jazz called China, who she knew was probably asleep already, too, because she just got off work.

After letting the phone go to voicemail three times, Jazz said, "Holla, bitch, when you get this. It's me."

Unable to reach anyone, her heart began to race, wondering what Fred's involvement was. Maybe he didn't pull the trigger, but China said he was with three new faces from out of town. *Damn, Fred!* First fuckin' China, and now conspiracy to murder. Oh, hell no! Not *her* Fred! She wasn't saving him secretly to be her baby's daddy for nothing. Prison for him was not an option, she swore. She just had to figure a way to ask Fred about it, but not let him know she knew he was around when it jumped off, nor about China. She had to call.

"Good morning, mister! Are you up yet?" Jazz asked.

"Yeah, I've been up for a while," Fred lied.

"Well, have you seen the news? Somebody got killed last night at Teasers."

"I came through there last night my damn self, and I seen a nigga get knocked out. One of my peoples had to check loudmouth-ass Stew. One of those niggas with him might've tried to bust in the air when we were leaving. I was out and know none of us let off. Girl, you know me. I play gangsta, but I don't do those murders. I ain't try'na kill nothing or let nothing die. Feel me?"

He continued. "They showed that little black motherfucka Stew on the news, too. He probably the main goddamn witness. He said the niggas that let off crazy and killed his man were in a black bulletproof car with New York plates. That nigga testified against his own cousin before, so you already know what's really good. It's not a game."

"True, I'm going to holla at my peoples and see what's good," Jazz said.

"For one, Stew tired. He gotta go to sleep. I got too much to lose for me to be sittin' up in San Dora. But yo, don't tell Mia, because it's 'bout to get ugly and she worries too much," he concluded.

******

D.B. had his head down, not wanting to believe the breaking news. Tears of disbelief rolled down his face. Still hung over, he began to blame himself for not looking out for his team. He didn't have a clue what to do. This was a part of the game no one told him about. April distracted him and his little head did all the thinking. It would only be a matter of time to hear from Stan because he always watched TV in the morning, and with a sketch of the twin, there'd be no denying it.

He felt betrayed because all last night they had a great time, and no one mentioned they had a situation. D.B. needed at least a day to think of something. He had to act normal so as not to alert anyone, including Escalade and City.

A call was placed immediately to One and Two, and they were to meet in an hour at their emergency spot – Stan's cabin in Valley Forge.

******

Stan checked his caller ID to see that Roger was calling. Being that it was before noon, this had to be good.

"What's up, bro-ham? I see your kind are at it again," Roger insultingly taunted.

"What in da hell you talking about now?" questioned Stan.

"Try murder at Teasers last night; and there's a witness and vehicle description. And, get this, the freakin' car was bulletproof. A local with a history witnessed everything – a little guy named

87

Steward Jones AKA Stew. An artist released a sketch already, and they're gonna be checking every armored detailing company in the tri-state area to get a lead on the vehicle. It was an Acura with New York plates."

"So, what happened?", Stan asked.

"It was an altercation which eventually led to gunplay, and the shooter had heavy firepower.", Roger said.

"This Steward fellow is the only reliable witness they have?"

"Everyone else probably was ducking for cover. I'd bet you lunch Steward actually knows one of the guys that was with the shooter. Unfortunately, there are no cameras in the club. Stew has a few things pending, though, so he'll cooperate. Hell, he told on his own cousin once to save his own ass; the rat bastard!", Roger yelled..

"Keep me posted and let's hope for an arrest for a change, instead of a 50-shot slaughter like New York.", Stan said.

"Yeah, right! In my book, the way I feel for someone who gets shot, I'd shoot the shooter. Now that's justice to me. Ever since my son was gunned down in cold blood, fuck 'em all!"

"I should've known," Stan said, hanging up the phone, thinking Roger was nothing more than a vigilante-ass racist with a police scanner.

Speed-dialing Douglas, Stan could barely stop his hand from trembling. How could the twins kill someone and no one contact him? He considered all of them family, especially since the twins lost their parents in a house fire, and D.B. was his nephew. There was no answer on either of their phone after several attempts.

This would be the most difficult time in all of their lives. Stan thought he taught them to be honest men that knew to do the right thing. Now the ball was in his court. Let his boys go down, knowing Roger's type would shoot on sight; or come up with a plan by all means necessary. This would include closing the eyes of their only witness. This is one time Roger could not win.

"It's family first. Fuck it!" he declared.

He thought hard as to where they could be. Drifting back to the years when they were growing up, one place they all could call home and loved so much was the cabin at Valley Forge. Stopping to grab a few items from his office, Stan was out the door in a hurry, bumping into a human brick wall.

Excusing himself, the man responded, "Everything criss," and kept it moving.

******

Finally reaching D.B., Escalade heard a cheerful, "What's up, boss? You just getting up?"

"Oh, hell no! You gotta be fuckin' kiddin' me! I just know you're not playing dumb with me. Have you heard the breaking news on every damn channel? Those fuckin' Philly niggas of yours – New York – whereva the fuck they from – they done killed a nigga last night when we was leaving the club, and ain't said jack shit to nobody! Niggas know me and my truck. City done knocked a nigga out that testified on his own cousin! Meanwhile, we trickin' like shit sweet. Where dey at? We gotta come up with a plan... *today!* I got peoples workin' at the prison, and I'm not trying to become their job security. Feel me? Those two bitches in the car with them saw something. Gotta holla at them, too, but I ain't going back to that club no time soon. So, what's the science, professor?"

"Yo, I heard just like you heard. I'm about to get with them now. I believe they got Denise and Keisha's numbers, too. Let me call you right back, or can you call China and see what's good?" D.B. asked.

"Yeah, I'll do that. In the meantime, get rid of that whip and we're all gonna play rentals. Holla back."

"Alright, boss, ten-four!"

"What?"

"Just trying to talk in code; Idaho style, you know?"

"Stupid motherfucka! Ten-four my ass!" Escalade mumbled as he hung up.

******

City was back in the Heights setting up shop by now. Big Wanda was distracting him with her sexy ass. The food smelled great coming from the kitchen, and lunch would soon be served.

Since he wasn't completely set up yet, he didn't have a television, and the radio played too many fast songs for the mood he wanted to set. He had *The Best of Jodeci* on CD on repeat.

Neither of them had a clue yet about what happened at the club, and with their cell phones turned off purposely, they decided only to share each other's nakedness for the remainder of the day.

# Chapter Fifteen

**Buenos Dias**

Lt. Larry was feeling rather talkative this evening. Perhaps the little sample he had sniffed – or was it the mega-blast he took in the parking lot – had him open.

With sweat beading on his forehead, he said to Malik, "*Sop-a-say*!" You'd assume he was trying to greet him in the Haitian tongue, except neither of them was from Haiti. He probably was leaning towards, "As-Salaam Alaikum!"

Malik took in his appearance and could see Lt. Larry was wide open.

"Yo, Malik, take this walk with me to my office to grab those pies I told you I'd bring."

Malik followed behind, and once he entered the office, he saw two fine-ass mommies in thongs and nail polish. Lt. Larry tried to introduce them, but the ladies had other plans.

Becca dropped to her knees and unleashed Malik's "night stick", licking just the tip as a sample.

Leeza began stripping Larry, telling no one in particular to lock the door.

Feeling the sensation of Becca's skillful suction, Malik had second thoughts about being in love with a mystery woman from the bus. Her beauty was overwhelming, and the skin contrast of light and dark made matters all the merrier.

Hearing Larry and Leeza fucking like crazy, Malik had to "spin the wheel". Pulling her thong to the side, he bent Becca over, ramming deep into her soul. They stroked and humped until he put her in the "bull man", which is when she's doggy style and he's on top with his legs on the outside, and his dick and balls are the only things in contact with her. She fucked him upwards, bucking her ass, and he had to balance and pound her with no hands, just like a bull ride. The added tension of balancing increases the explosion.

Larry, on the other hand, must have forgotten that he and Lisa were not in the room alone. He broke out with, "Oh, Leeza, in my ass! Yes, fuck my hot ass!" and there was a buzzing sound.

That kind of blew the moment for Malik, so he and Becca began gathering themselves.

After a few more grunts, Larry exploded, breathing and sweating like crazy.

"Well, I see you two met," he said. "I told you she'd put it on you. Wait 'til you try both of them. They'll have you cuttin' your dreads!" Larry laughed.

"It ain't the time for that. It's more about this real business for now. We can have pleasure later. Feel me?"

"Well I'm sure you heard how we get down," said Leeza. "We're down for whatever, especially when it's about this paper. You might can't buy love, but I know you can at least buy a lot of 'like'!"

"Real talk, I need y'all on my team. I just got back, and I'm not here that long. But what we can do is make enough money to live lovely. I mean better than ever. There's going to be some changes and expansions. Are you in?" asked Malik.

They both weren't sure if this new business would interfere or cause conflict with their present moves.

Before they could ask, Malik informed them, "Shit is about

to go down. I mean, from the warden to some of your present crew. Everything isn't what it appears. Luckily, we have inside information to help us combat the problems before it bites us all in the ass.

"For example," he continued, "you already make moves for Akbar and Snow White. Akbar is down with me and the Gods. However, he's not as hard as he appears. Right, Larry?"

"Oh, he gets quite hard from what I seen!" Larry responded, laughing.

"Well, we have new connects and bigger opportunities to get paid. Larry said you're real, so can I count on you?" Malik waited for an answer.

Both agreed. "Yeah, papi, no problema!"

For now, they agreed to remain on third shift and in their normal positions, such as outside towers or hospital security. Yet, they would move more cash out of the bing and stash more weight than before. With more new customers, there'd be a greater need for a larger supply on hand.

******

Already the following night, Becca was flirting with Akbar, and she told him to be ready at about two. He was to play sick, and she'd escort him supposedly to the hospital. Instead, he thought he'd finally get to fuck her, but he got fucked!

They pulled over, and she uncuffed one handcuff while inside the car. She instructed him to get out, and they'd fuck on the hood of the car.

From being locked up for so long, Akbar didn't realize security vehicles were equipped with cameras on the front, and when he walked in front of the vehicle with one cuff dangling, it would look undoubtedly like an escape, giving her the right to shoot to kill.

With one shot to the head and a stack of paperwork to follow, Akbar's death and attempted escape actually didn't surprise the Gods or authorities. He still had quite some time to go, but Born had a feeling Malik just hurried him up.

# Chapter Sixteen

**Goodnight, Stew!**

Escalade kept his regular routine and picked up more work and dropped the cash off to Jazz as normal. She loved Fred and figured that morning would be a perfect time to show it since Mia wasn't around. So, after packaging the "shit" and stashing the money, she told Fred not to go so fast.

He looked baffled, but as her full-length robe revealed her hot flesh, Fred no longer was in a hurry to leave.

Their embrace was like a "clash of the titans" – fingers running through hair, bodies grinding hard, moans escalating into loudness. A pile of rags formed, and like a mountain of love, they were on top, licking, sucking, and biting.

Fred was everything inside of her that she hoped and longed for, and then some. The only form of protection they used was locked doors. No matter! She wanted his seed to swim deep up in her.

Fred was going to become, right then and there, her baby-daddy. Just as she lived, it was not an option. Grabbing his ass, she pulled him in even deeper, wrapping her legs around his back as she felt the squirting of love saturate her zone.

Exploding with a smile, she kissed him, saying "Thank you, baby-daddy!"

To her surprise, Fred responded, "You're welcome, baby-momma!" not minding truthfully if Jazz got pregnant the first time they made love.

Fred still had to find out what was going on with his crew and told Jazz they'd talk later.

Jazz had her own plans, and knew exactly what had to happen.

******

Stew, meanwhile, was at a mobile interrogation center spilling his guts to the "alphabet boys" (FBI).

"The main two niggas that I know are City and Escalade, but the niggas with them ain't from around here. I heard City's shit got raided just the other day, and the police clapped his man. He probably fuckin' with Escalade now because he got the One Way on smash."

Special Agent Roger Hawkins handed Stew a pre-programmed cell phone with his direct number on speed dial, an iced-out watch that was a listening device, and a throw-away pistol.

Stew looked surprised until Roger said, "Come on. We know you guys carry – what ya call it– temperatures?"

"Naw, man. We carry 'heat'," Stew said, telling on his damn self.

Roger proved his theory: If you want to know something, just ask a nigger!

Jotting down the two names given, Agent Hawkins was certain to begin his investigation strong. He sent Steward on his way with $500, which doesn't seem like much. However, Steward got a free pass to hustle in the hood, and that was the real fringe benefit of snitching. Real talk, the love of money and the lack of power and respect got the game twisted!

******

Escalade was still waiting to hear from D.B., so to kill time he stopped by the head shop. Just as he hoped, his favorite cashier was there.

"Um, how may I help you, Little Pockets?" she joked.

"You the cashier, bitch!" Fred spat his venom. "And check carreerbuilders.com before you try'na play me. I got what will make you complete," he said, pointing first to her and then to himself. "Fish and chips!" he added, laughing at his own shit.

"Like Cheryl Underwood said, 'You're like giving a Tic-Tac to a whale', you fake-ass Nas on some street dreams, but they made of these," she said, slamming down her black card.

Escalade was shocked and impressed. Not just how she did it, but what she said afterward was some classic Gouldtown, New Jersey slang from '79-'80.

She said, "Nutted your panties!"

For a minute, Escalade went back to the pre-VCR days when legends were born daily, having been told some Longview Drive niggas playing basketball started that saying. It was today's equivalent to "In your face!" or a "Now what, bitch-ass nigga?" dis. Those were *real* niggas back in the days, he'd been told. Now it was all new-school, burying each other. Whatever happened to being cool and talking junk, trying to live?

"Is everything okay?" Tina asked, causing Escalade to drift back.

"Yeah, I'm fine. It was just something you said."

"What was that?" she asked.

"That old-school slang you used. My peoples invented that," Escalade boasted.

"Whatever!" she smiled. "Anyways, I own this store and five others throughout the state. I bet you never knew I own the Wish-wash, too. Y'all niggas just call it 'The Wash' or 'The Water'."

"And how old are you?" Fred asked.

"I'm twenty-two, and married young into money. Ain't no need to be fuckin' for peanuts when you can fuck for the elephant!" she laughed.

96

"True, true. Maybe we can do business one day. Be easy!" he said, walking out the door, feeling defeated.

******

Steward felt like the world was just at his fingertips for the taking, or at least the city, for that matter. Little did he know, Jazz was a *true* C.O. She'd correct everything as soon as she saw him.

Putting on a regular pair of sweat pants and hoody, she went into the living room closet and withdrew a black revolver, .357 snub. With no need to discuss anything with anyone, once again, it was on!

Jazz turned a few corners and bent a few lanes trying to spot Stew. Passing the Wish-wash, she spotted the nigga running his mouth. As usual, she parked unnoticed down the block and scoped everything out from her rearview mirror. It was too crowded for her to run up on him, so she just waited.

Finally, he pulled off alone, headed right in her direction. With her engine already running, she followed him like a shadow, waiting for him to slip. As he turned into the self-serve gas station, which looked like a ghost town, she parked and timed his fatal error.

Exiting her car from around the block, she tightened her hoody and began jogging right in his direction. Being that Jazz was hood, she knew most niggas filled up their whips before nightfall to avoid getting out of their cars when it was dark.

Stew pumped his gas while bopping his head to "Many men, many, many, many men wish…"

*"By-yaw! By-yaw!"* went the gun as she dumped into him, not missing a stride. The first shot to the body caused blood and gas to leak everywhere. Apparently, his hand was locked onto the nozzle in shock. The second shot to the face made him kiss the devil.

Jazz busted a U-turn and headed back, jogging to her car, but not before lickin' one shot to the concrete, kicking a spark which caused an inferno.

Time was flying, and in less than an hour and a half, it would be time for work. She thought to herself, *This is the one thing I was born for, being a correctional officer to the fullest—'Bout it!*

## Chapter Seventeen

### Home Away From Home

Valley Forge was always a place in the Fall to find peace. However, this time, D.B. was on the warpath, looking for answers. In disbelief, they all shook their heads, hoping to be awakened from such a horrific nightmare.

"My bad, y'all. I was drunk as hell and didn't know what the hell made me flip. I guess hearing the gunshots and seeing the fire come out of their heat made me go bananas."

D.B. snapped. "Bullshit! Try again! You wasn't drivin' and your alter-ego here pulled over so you could get out and start shooting! Correct me if I'm wrong."

"Yeah," said One, "but I was drunk, too!"

"I don't believe you two identical liars. Do you realize someone is dead and there's a witness?"

"*Was* a witness," Two said with a smile, while pointing to the TV with breaking news.

Now if they weren't there with him, D.B. would have sworn they killed the witness, too. Escalade wasn't built for that, and City never left the Heights, so he thought.

One had jokes. "Well, since there's no witness, we won't have to explain our positions to Stan or blow up our spot with Escalade or City."

"We're not out of the woods yet, because Stan is still going to have a cow. How are we going to explain the black Acura with New York plates? We could say it wasn't us, but he designed the car and knows it's bulletproof," D.B. reminded them.

Two said, "I got us into this, so I'll get us out. When everything hits the fan, we'll blame City for the homicide. Hell, with two drug factories operating simultaneously, that's life anyway, and it's not telling; it's baseball – three strikes and you're out!"

D.B. hated to lie, but this was one time the truth wouldn't set them free.

"Two, wasn't D.B. enjoying himself last night?"

"Hell yeah! He was grittin' his teeth like a motherfucka! He was rollin'!"

"That's it! That's it!" D.B. screamed. "One of those bitches put something in the drinks. I bet we were really rollin' last night for real. That's how we ended up at the Turnpike, butt-ass naked, trickin'. Stan would have had our heads for that shit!"

"Bullshit! Stan would have had *your* head. We were answering a call—a call of nature, that is!" They both laughed uncontrollably.

Getting back into focus, they ironed out their story to tell Escalade and City lies, but on the side, telling Stan more lies, too. No one wanted to hear his mouth just yet, they decided.

******

By now, Special Agent Hawkins knew it was Stew from the license plate and cell phone lying at a distance from the blaze. That's what was left of it. All along he didn't realize the close connection to Stan this case really had. Would he ever know now?

******

Mia and Jazz went to work on time expecting the usual. I guess secrets are good, and they both were keeping them.

Jazz made her moves, dropping off and collecting, while Mia studied the notebook. Actually, she'd been getting into the pro Blackness of it all. To her, it made more sense than anything she'd ever read.

Hearing keys, Mia looked up to see the captain headed her way. She stashed the notebook in the empty cell and stood, acting as if she were observing the accuracy of her watch compared to the clock on the wall.

Captain Davis she only saw once, and he more or less was by-the-book. He signed in the log and kept it moving, directing a new inmate in her direction. It was a little red-headed white boy. He had to be grown, but his size made him boyish compared to the other men. He went to his cell and she locked the door, wondering how the hell to add him to the count.

By the time Jazz came back, all she had to do was show Mia how to do the paperwork. Other than that, business was good, and "you-know-who" was due for a piss break.

Forgetting all about the notebook, Mia headed straight to Brianna's cell. "Hey, girlfriend!" she called.

"Aren't we cute today?" Brianna responded.

"You wanna watch? Sike!"

"See, you ain't right! Anyways, how you doin'?"

They both laughed.

While Mia pissed and was about to head back, Brianna, out of the blue, said, "Be careful and don't do nothing you'd regret, girlfriend."

That was kind of strange, but heartfelt, because Mia gave this drug business some thought. To her, she'd rather have the guy from the bus and love rather than drug money any day.

****** 

Stan wanted to see who in the hell was who, by phone. D.B. had convinced him to play it cool and act like he was just their gun connect and had a chop shop to get rid of the black Acura.

Inside the sparsely furnished Heights apartment, everyone shied away from details about anything.

As Stan was leaving, he thought he recognized City, but wasn't sure from where. He knew they'd met before for sure once.

He asked him, "How's everything?"

City answered, "Everything criss!"

******

Jazz never even noticed that Akbar wasn't around the entire shift, nor did Snow White. *There's too many fuckin' secrets,* she thought, but didn't dwell on it because they could've been anywhere in the jail.

What was happening was a perfect crime being understandable for all points and purposes – or else!

Although the shooting appeared justifiable, the warden had to consider the outcome once the news and the prisoners got wind of it. Yeah, yeah, yeah, he realized he did attempt to escape. Then he held that thought, because no way in hell was a Puerto Rican woman C.O. gonna kill one of the Gods at two-something a.m., talking about in route to the hospital. No one would have fallen for that, so he pressured Snow White to say it was a heart attack to keep the peace and business, as usual.

Emotional moves caused huge mistakes, and the warden didn't appreciate the fact that someone had the balls to pay someone who was technically his employee to commit a murder while on his watch.

"Never did care for Mexican bitches!" he pouted.

This was far from over, because it could mess up his system of doing things, and he'd transfer or get to killing himself before that happened.

******

Heading to the parking lot, Mia and Jazz spotted Snow walking with her head down, wiping her eyes. They approached, concerned for their friend.

"Hey, girl, where have you been all day? In the dorms?"

"I wish!" she replied, sniffling and wiping her eyes.

Mia opened her arms, signaling for a hug. "What's the matter?"

Snow broke down right there in the parking lot to a point that Jazz had to help grab her.

"Akbar is dead! My man is dead! Somebody killed him. Somebody murdered him! Fuck this place! Fuck this job and fuck the warden! Everybody's gonna pay for this shit. Watch! He got the nerve to tell me he'll pay me to say he died of natural causes. But since when do gunshot wounds become part of the human anatomy? I gotta go!" She forcefully broke away.

"Wait!"

"I'm fine," she said, slamming her car door and squealing off full of rage.

"Damn!" was all that could be said as they sat in the car, speechless.

"This job is more than I thought, Jazz. Shit, being a C.O. is some real shit, I see. How in the fuck you get shot in jail? That's the fuck it! I should've been a stripper. I wouldn't have minded giving a little head. That's better than working here and getting my whole head knocked da fuck off."

"Girl, who you tellin'? I need a drink after all this bullshit. Fuck! And you heard what that bitch said, right? That *everybody's* gonna pay. Shit!"

"It's her nature."

"Goddamn white girl chasing dick and ready to fuck up everybody's good thing because she mad over a nigga's head gettin' smacked off."

"Crackers be on some shit. They get mad and tell on you and their damn selves!"

"She can't get no props and be called a cracker, because that's what the slaves nicknamed the master because he cracked the whip. She's a white bitch, though, all day.

"She about to be a dead bitch!" Jazz said.

With that said, the ride home was quiet. Mia planned on going home to call Snow to make sure she was okay. Jazz went home to plan her next move.

Mia, being the softer of the two, was no fool by far, and wasn't trying to become no bitch's bitch down the road.

Both were curious to know what was said in the warden's office, what his involvement was, and the course of action planned. Also, what kind of hell was about to break loose at work tomorrow once word got out to the Gods.

# Chapter Eighteen

**Double Time**

That very night, Warden Brown prepared to clean house once and for all. It was time he flexed his muscles, because things had gotten way out of hand. He needed answers, and "I don't knows" would get a motherfucker killed.

First, he needed his most trusted staff informed of the mishap. Then again, he realized that several of his prisoners knew how to dispose of a body. Perhaps a substantially reduced sentence, with cash plus benefits, would do the trick. All movement had to stop and all communication to and from the outside had to cease.

Then an ingenious plan popped into his head: *Pull the plug!* He would say Akbar escaped and was at large, but tell Lt. Larry to leak out to the Gods that Snow White was going to the Feds because she found out Ak' was gay and had run off with a former cellmate of his.

Brilliant! But, not so fast!

The entire shift was held over and second shift had to come

in early for a double. The alarm sounded just before prayer call. San Dora was officially on Code Red – lockdown.

******

The media was buzzing outside of the entrance gates, but no one said anything because they knew nothing.

Snow White did a no-show, and Mia was unsuccessful in reaching her. No one knew about their conversation in the parking lot, or so they thought.

Warden Brown was on his "A" game. He'd done his homework, and thanks to the parking lot surveillance tapes, he needed to remind Jazz and Mia that whatever was said needed to be forgotten.

"Well, ladies, what do we have here? One of two things: Either a plus or a problem. You see, whatever she told you in the parking lot can either be worth a lot or worthless to you. My sisters," he said, playing the race card, "white bitches are dumb because she attempted to blow the whistle and tell on all of us."

"All of us?" Mia asked innocently enough.

"Yes, all of us. I had her wires tapped at home for months, and when she placed the call to the Feds as promised, by talking to her kind, she thought she'd be safe. However, a dear friend of mine was waiting for her call. As we speak, let's just say she's tied up at the moment."

"Now, Mia," he continued, "you've been here about a week, and you're looking at life in prison for breach of security to the State. You perjured yourself by violating your oath, and you've compiled a host of drug charges. Did you know that a camera's lens can be about as small as the eye of a needle nowadays, if not smaller?

"Oh, and Jazz, did you ever check your car for sound? I did, especially for rainy days just like this. Just as DMX said, 'When it rains, niggas get wet!' So, ladies, is there a problem or a plus?"

Saying nothing, they looked dazed.

"Let me continue then, because I don't believe we're clear here. Jazz, haven't you been a busy bee on my clock, in my facility.

The nerve of you! Tell me, did you lose your mind? No way in hell did you think you were going to sell drugs and pussy and I not get mines! I should just smack the shit out of you! Oh, and I guess you know, if we *ever* have a problem, MySpace will get a free "C.O.'s Gone Wild" video of your ass in rare form.

"Poor Mia! My poor darling Mia. You're quite the freak late night on the phone, aren't we?"

Not wanting Jazz to know, Mia spoke up. "What is it you want from us? There is no problem. It's a plus with us. I don't know her like that."

"Could have fooled me," he said, dying to let the cat out of the bag.

Jazz added, "I don't have a problem. Fuck Akbar and the white bitch. And I'ma give you some of this pussy, for real. I can see myself being a captain, 'cause after I put it on you and make it clap, you'll be all set, buddy boy!"

"Say when!" Brown said, excited.

Regardless of the chaotic situation, a dog is a dog, and a bitch is a bitch. After viewing so many episodes of Jazz's "sexcapades", that had to be some fire, he thought.

Before leaving his office, they planned to do lunch and finish sorting this mess out. They promised to say nothing, and actually, they were in no position because of the leverage and pressure the warden applied.

Relieving some guy from third shift, they just sat in the bubble with nothing left but exhaustion.

"We're screwed! Faggot motherfucka said he should smack the shit out of me! He just don't know. I would've blew his top right the fuck off. I stay strapped. I bet his little cameras and microphones didn't let him know that!" Jazz said.

"Word, girl! He must be on some shit! Warden or not, if that motherfucka would've touched you, we would have jumped his raggedy old ass!"

"He can't even handle this good pussy, and I don't need no AIDS! Fucking homo! Mia, are you going to be good for a few? I'm about to let Born know what's going on."

"How? We're not supposed to say nothing," Mia whined.

"Girl, my nickname should've been 'Sealy Posturepedic' the way I be catching bodies. Warden Brown is a dead motherfucka. I ain't trusting no nigga to have secrets on me. I wouldn't give a fuck about showing my ass on the Internet. You still new to all of this, but if you look in the back of XXL, you'd see how hoes be taking nude and panty shots and sending them up the way. Well, with contacts and a little weave, my ass is like Connecticut prisons – everywhere serving niggas! Pussy is powerful, and it's not hard to get a murderer to kill again, especially once you satisfy his weakness."

"Jazz, let me go piss before you go. I'll be real quick," Mia said, running off.

Brianna was sitting up with a sad look on her face. But she couldn't have known anything, being locked all night, Mia thought.

Brianna forced herself to say, "How you doin'?"

"I'm not," Mia said.

"Yeah, I know."

"Know what?"

"I saw and overheard Ms. B. setting Akbar up the night before last. When he didn't come back, I knew it was a wrap. You know how you can look at a bitch's body language and see the phoniness? I got a picture of them leaving his cell with his hand all over her ass. See?"

"Damn, girlfriend! You be on the case!"

"What's the warden saying?"

"Not too much," Mia lied.

"Call down and see if he wants me to come to work. His freaky ass can't tell all of this 'no'!" Brianna said, twirling around.

"Good idea. Let me tell Jazz and get right back to you."

"Okay, be safe."

Mia quickly told Jazz about the picture Brianna took with her cell phone, and how she'd go to work and be eyes and ears for them. "I told her it was up to you, but definitely a good idea."

"Let me go talk to Born first real quick, and I'll just walk her to his office as a surprise to him. I'll tell him we thought he could use a little eye candy," Jazz said.

******

Born was up and wondered what was going on. The other officer told everyone there was a fight in the dorm and a makeshift weapon was involved, calling for a Code Red. Born was not buying that one bit. From experience, it cost the State too much in overtime to pay double time for a makeshift weapon.

"Ms. J., they act like somebody got shot and died."

"Born, baby, listen carefully," she said, reaching to caress his hands. "On my word, somebody did get shot and died. Akbar is dead. That's why we didn't see him at all yesterday, and Snow White is missing."

"How did he die?"

"He got shot!"

"In jail? How in the hell you get shot in jail? Now this is some bullshit! Astafallah!"

"Brianna has a picture on her phone of Akbar leaving his cell hugged up with Ms. B. from third shift."

"The Mexican bitch?"

"She's not Mexican. She's just a big-face Puerto Rican."

"That still don't prove he's dead or got shot."

"Snow told me that the warden had a full report and dash cam video of Akbar trying to escape while in route to the hospital for emergency treatment. Ms. B. had to use deadly force, or so she said. But the warden didn't believe that bullshit. He wanted Snow White to tell everyone Ak' died of a heart attack so there'd be no investigation. Plus, he wasn't signing for no autopsy. You know Snow White was dick whipped, and the devil came out of her. We caught her leaving in the parking lot, and her last words were, 'Everybody's gonna pay'."

"Pay how?"

"She called the Feds when she got home, but Warden Brown was on his 'A' game. He had her wires tapped months ago for days like this."

"So what happened?"

"One of his butt-buddies is a fed and intercepted her anticipated call. Being that he was a white agent, she easily fell for the trap. She went to meet him somewhere, and the warden left it like, 'She's tied up at the moment'."

"What's the plan?"

"I'm taking my secret weapon, Brianna, in to keep the warden company, and Mia and I are supposed to have lunch with him to discuss where we go from here."

"I say we need to be off lockdown to not attract outside attention. Plus, I need movement to feel right. How's my man Malik in the dorm?"

"I'll check right after lunch and get everyone off lockdown, or pop you out regardless. Let momma handle this, okay?"

"Okay, Jazz. Yeah, I like the sound of that!"

"Oh, and smile, because everywhere around here we've been on 'Candid Camera'—naked, too! Shit, the warden said we're one keystroke away from Myspace, but he can dot-com my whole ass. I'ma see you after lunch."

Returning to the bubble, Jazz updated Mia on their conversation, and the one good point was to take everyone off lockdown so it wouldn't look so suspicious, like Born suggested.

"Go see if Brianna's ready, and I'll walk her down and let her work her magic," Jazz said.

# Chapter Nineteen

**Special Report**

In the Heights, no one knew what to think, except they were very lucky that things turned out the way they did. Big Wanda had assured all of them that her crew was built for anything, regardless.

After Stan had left to dispose of the car, Escalade brought in a housewarming gift for City – one mainly for himself. The plasma TV came in handy, because with so much going on, they all wanted to keep up with the news at noon.

With old habits being hard to break, most people still watched the dumb-ass "Price is Right" and then the twelve o'clock news after that. Everyone in the hood fascinated about spinning the wheel and winning both showcases.

Now, before the second showcase showdown could finish, a news flash put the brakes on everything.

"We interrupt our regularly scheduled programming to bring you a live special report: A heavily guarded San Dora, New Jersey State Prison has been on Code Red – lockdown, since approximately 5:45 this morning. Outside, media frenzy has begun. We take you live to the front gates of what New Jerseites call 'the gates of hell', with Shamik Shatanae reporting."

"Thanks, Shekeem. Well, right now there has been no actual word of what's really going on inside. A call was placed to the governor's mansion, and we're awaiting comment. You see, a Code Red calls for double staff and double time. No one is allowed to leave until the investigation subsides to at least a Code Yellow. Good thing the weather is not so cold, because I'll be right here to bring you the latest news. Shekeem, back to you."

"Thank you, Shamik. Well, it looks like whatever happened is pretty serious, and just to put it out there, if any C.O.'s just happen to call our station exclusively and privy us as to what's going on, we just might have season passes for four to see the Giants.

"I'm Shekeem Harold, reporting for Channel 77 News."

"Oh, shit! My little sister just started working there last week, and my girl has been there for about two years," Escalade continued. "There's a lot of bullshit going on up in there."

"Like what?" D.B. asked.

"Shit, you ain't know? I got more yay movin' in there than we do out here. My girl and my sister got a whole crew of C.O.'s doing the damn thing."

This caught everyone's attention. D.B., One, Two, and City couldn't believe their ears and wanted to know more.

"I na no my yoot, hear mi say. So you tell me da police gal an dem run da drug t'ing in a prison?" City asked, and then sucked his teeth. "Mi doubt dat, bredren. Dem God-body boys a run t'ings. You not see it."

Escalade, on the offensive, went Ja-fake'in to prove to City that he didn't know jack shit.

"Hey, boy. Wha ya talk so an not say nuttin'? Ya t'ink me play win me play? A me dis Escalade da missin' link to all dem boy dat! Wha ya t'ink dem boy re-up upon da commissary list? Wha ya t'ink, dem boy do, open da mail and out pop a blood clot key of coke? Idiot boy, now hear me say, dis da real t'ing, muthafucka!"

All you heard after that was, "Wow!"

In everyone's mind, things were deeper than they thought. Hell, things were deeper than they imagined. They all tried to piece some of these strange events together.

D.B. had to press for more details, but ask his questions nonchalantly.

City couldn't wait for everyone to leave so he could go and report what he just heard.

The twins were still relieved about the witness, Stew, being taken care of.

Escalade decided they all would take a break until he heard from Mia and Jazz. By saying their names, he might as well have been standing in quicksand, sinking his empire fast.

# Chapter Twenty

## Eye Candy

When Jazz and Brianna walked into the warden's office, his eyes grew to the size of saucers.

"Well, well! This is unexpected," he stammered. "Is it my birthday, or did I die and go to heaven?" he laughed.

"Since lunch is still two hours away, I thought you could use a little eye candy. Plus, afterwards, you know we're going to have to shift some money around, and we'll need your computer because it's the fastest. See, I think a*head*, and give it wickedly!" Jazz finished, licking her lips before leaving.

Brianna, on the other hand, was wondering why Jazz would even get this nigga started. Then the plan popped in her head. She'd have the warden get nice, and she'd pour the first round and let him pour the second, knowing he'd spike her drink again. However, this time, she'd switch glasses without him knowing!

"So we have two hours. What's on the agenda?" the warden asked.

"You already know. I'm try'na get nice. I've been in that hot, tight hole and I need to get loose." Brianna chose some very enticing words. "I know you have some toot. I'll pour the first round."

Just as planned, the warden was walking right into the trap. Brianna made sure to give him a lot of ass shots and cleavage.

Swirling the ice cubes with her finger and extending it for the warden to lick off, he insisted, "Call me Brownie."

"Okay, Brownie. What in the hell is going on? I was just loving life and about to step my game up. Nobody had to tell me anything. I saw Ms. B. leave with Akbar, and when he didn't come back, I knew it was a wrap," she said, then took a sip.

"What kills me is who put her up to it. She's kind of new still, but that damn Leeza probably had something to do with it. We'll see at lunch time," the warden said.

"That we will, because they fuckin' with business—*my* business, and I know you want me happy, Brownie."

Reaching for her glass, the warden went for the refill. Brianna purposely went to adjust the stereo's volume to give "Brownie" plenty of time to make his move. He did just as expected and became all too excited with himself.

"Look at that!" Brianna teased, pointing to the slight bulge in his pants. "Come dance with me. The drinks ain't going anywhere. Hurry, because this is my song."

"*You's a big fine woman...why don't you back dat ass up...,*" played.

Brianna backed it up on his ass, too! Remembering which glass he had extended to her originally, she made the switch and watched him gulp it straight down, which would subconsciously suggest to Brianna to guzzle hers, as well, but she had other plans.

"We still have about an hour and a half. I know you have some movies we can watch. I'm in the mood for something sort of erotic. Just a little something to get the ole oils flowing, you know the, ah, coffee percolating."

"Say no more! I am the erotic king!" he bragged. "I've actually starred in a few myself."

"Ew! Brownie, you're just too much for me!"

"That's what they all say," he remarked, while grabbing his nuts.

Faking like the drink began taking effect, Brianna slouched on the couch. Brownie couldn't move fast enough, hurrying himself, now knowing he was the one starting to go under.

"Relax and take that off. Momma got plans for you!" she said, reaching for the bulge in his pants.

As he sat back and started drifting, the rage started boiling inside of Brian. No longer waiting for the drink to completely control the situation, Brian hauled off and punched the warden once in the temple/eye area, and he was out for the count.

Instinct and training kicked into high gear. First, he needed to secure the area, and then track down the surveillance apparatus. This was one tape that would never be viewed.

Warden Brown was handcuffed and gagged for the moment, while Brian continued on his mission. Using an AM/FM portable radio, "Detective Brian St. John, of the New Jersey State Police" made an electronic wand and vigorously swept the office for sound breach.

Rapidly tracing wires, he discovered an entire secret panel that covered the brainchild to all of his audio/visual horrors. There were several discs to confiscate, and one to be permanently destroyed. With unbelievable luck, everything was in alphabetical order. "Brianna" was second row, third in.

Quickly popping the disc in to make certain of the inevitable, Brian lost it. Ripping the disc out and cracking it up into several pieces, he threw it in the plastic garbage pail and reached for a lighter. Flicking only once, the disc began to melt as the trash burned away his assault.

The office had some smoke, so Brian opened the window and shifted a fan to accommodate the situation.

Rushing to the computer, he typed in, "Mr. AWS said hello" and instant messaged it straight to Governor Gary Nulls. This was a private password with "SWARM' being spelled backwards, signaling twelve hours to send in the troops. "Hey, it's New Jersey

AKA New Jerusalem."

Detective Brian St. John also majored in computer design and discovered a way to transfer an entire brain and memory outward, while truly erasing all history permanently. And that he did to later sort out the wealth. After all, being undercover for over a year, bad habits tend to become contagious, especially involving millions.

With Brown still out, but only moments away from lunch, the detective had to think fast. In twelve hours, his entire case would meet its end.

Mia and Jazz really became dear to him. They were real, and although he was a fraud, he could relate to their kindness and greed. He thought, if only to save them, and most of the money, everyone would live happily ever after. So, back undercover he went.

******

"Sure is smoky in here!" Mia said, referring to the lonely corridor leading to the warden's office.

"Yeah," Jazz responded. "Brianna must have really been dropping it like it's hot!" she said, laughing at her own joke.

As they neared the door, the scent of burnt debris was evident. Jazz sped up, trying to turn the knob to a locked door.

Knocking, she let out a sigh of relief once she heard Brianna say, "Who?"

"It's me and Mia," Jazz answered.

Upon entering the smoky office, they couldn't help but notice Warden Brown laid out in handcuffs, with a black eye and a lump the size of a golf ball protruding from his brow.

"Damn, I thought you were the eye candy, but it looks to me like you gave him a 'Now-or-Later'! What the fuck happened? And I need a *drank*, 'cause a *drink* is too small! I'm not quenching no thirst; a bitch is try'na feel it!"

Helping herself to the open liquor cabinet, Jazz took a big swig straight from the bottle. "Mia, make sure that door is locked, and open some more windows, Brianna. I'm about to choke in this bitch! Okay, tell me something," Jazz said, referring to Brianna.

117

"Well, I was trying to get some scoop, while he was steady trying to get some. He tried to get 'brawlic' and called himself smacking the shit out of somebody. Before I knew it, I did the 'Matrix' on his raggedy ass and took him to the tiles. Shit, he's lucky we wasn't on concrete, but his back won't know the difference. I flipped that nigga so fast and then touched him up with a few quick power blows. You would've thought Bruce Leroy done finally got at Sho' Nuff!"

"It's gotta be the shoes!" Jazz busted out, laughing about the jail-issued sneakers that looked like kung fu shoes.

"What are we going to do when he wakes up?" Mia asked.

"I don't know. But before he does, I'm going to dot his other eye for him, since his freaky ass always likes spying. Now see this?" Jazz said to an unconscious Warden Brown, and then punched him so hard in the other eye that she hurt her own hand.

Mia joined in. "Fuck it! Since he likes running his mouth..." She did a roundhouse and both his lips began bleeding, while his shattered dentures flew all over the room.

Brianna tried to regain order, knowing that the clock was ticking. "Ladies, don't kill him yet. We'll get one of the lifers to do it. They'll enjoy that, I'm sure. I did find all the tapes and discs he had stored in his little secret lair. Look!"

"Damn, he had an entire library of footage, and I'm burning all of this shit up today!" Jazz swore.

The warden really didn't know why Akbar got murdered, and they needed to find out. Becca was a new jack and wasn't doing shit without Leeza and Lt. Larry, they figured.

"I'll call over to the dorm and get them over here ASAP," Jazz assured them. "Put his ass in the bathroom and wipe this blood up. We'll say he's in the lounge resting for a minute, if they ask."

Ten minutes later in walked Lt. Larry, C.O. Leeza, and C.O. Becca.

The ladies did their special handshake, asking, "Is you 'bout it?" and ended with balled fists touching knuckles and turning in a circular motion.

"I'm 'bout it, 'bout it!"

"Enough of this shit, sweethearts. Can someone fill a bitch in, too? We're all ladies here," Lt. Larry said.

"Well, I'm sure by now all of us know we have several things in common besides where we work. I'm referring to all of our illegal activities we indulge in especially. I know we're all real, so everybody can speak for themselves. The main thing right now is Akbar's been shot, and Becca, you let him out of his cell, and for whatever dumb-ass reason, shot him up, and his bitch, Snow White, tried going to the Feds to tell on everyone."

"The warden has been on his 'A' game stronger than we thought. He knew long ago she'd be a weak link, and had her wires tapped months ago. So when she called to tell it all, she ended up meeting an agent who was down with the program all along. I don't know where she's at. We had to pound the warden's ass out, and he's in the bathroom, cuffed."

Pulling out her pistol, Jazz continued. "Nobody play hero, and we're good. But one of you is going to tell me who put Becca up to kill Akbar. However, if you lie, ya die! And so much of my money and product is fucked up now. Think I give a fuck? *Not*!"

The sound of a mouse pissin' on cotton could be heard. For Jazz to be so loving, she was a natural born killer. By just being in the room, you could smell her blood boiling in her veins. Her hand was too steady for this to be a first time. Jazz was 'bout it, 'bout it!

Becca had heart and understood this wasn't a direct challenge from Jazz or Mia. She understood that her actions and greed for fifty G's just fucked up everybody's money and way of doing business in the bing forever. So, she began with the truth, remembering Jazz's promise, "You lie, ya die!"

"Okay, mommy. I met a Malik. We fuck around, mommy, *poquito*. He told me Akbar bad for a business. I choot 'em and he giv'a me fiddy gee's. I tell the warden I have him on a camera trying to escapee, and run to fight with me. I don't know. The warden have paper works, and I have my monies. Sorry, mommy. Lt. Larry let me meet him, so I think everybody's okay."

In his defense, Lt. Larry said, "I introduced y'all because he has the kane and was expanding operations. I knew there were to be some changes made, but no killing. Shit! I like flowers, the colors pink and purple, and rainbow Skittles. I have Teletubbies tapes, and I puke at the sight of blood. I got so much sugar in my tank, my daddy's named Domino and my mother is Mrs. Butterworth! Bitch, you must like carrots, because you're out of your rabbit-ass mind to think I'm down with murder. I do freaky shit, not dumb shit. I'm happier than two faggots with a bag of dicks. I ain't around!"

"Alrightee then!" Brianna said. "I guess you've cleared your name. I just have a few questions for clarity's sake. What Malik are you talking about? Is this the Malik that is best friends with Born Freedom? Well, somebody say something!"

Lt. Larry said, "Yes, it is. I know Malik and how he operates. I bet Born doesn't even know the real deal. Out of the two, it's night and day, just depending on the situation. Both are good people and both are deadly."

"We're about to get to the bottom of this mess right now. Here, Brianna. If any of these three stooges move, burn their asses. Mia, go get Born and tell him I went to the dorm to get Malik. Radio me if there's a problem," Jazz said before rushing off.

# Chapter Twenty-One

## Surprise, Surprise!

Everyone went about their own business. Escalade stared at his phone, hoping it would ring. Worried about Mia and Jazz, he had no place to turn except to the sky.

"O, Allah, I submit, forgive me for my wrongdoings and please bring them out of this alive. I'll quit everything, knowing you have the power. Amen!"

With that said, he walked slowly into the store, bought a water, and slowly walked out to be confronted by a homeless man.

"My brother, can you spare some change?" said the man.

Escalade looked at him, and for the first time in his life, he imagined how this guy must feel to have nothing or no one. As a lonely tear spilled onto his cheek, he reached in his pocket and pulled out the infamous Chinese bankroll, and in another pocket, pure hundreds.

Reaching out, Escalade said, "Brother, my name is Fred, and this is for you," then handed him all the money.

The old homeless man shouted, "Allah Akbar and Jazakallah!

121

If you ever need anything and its fisabilallah, I'm there for you, Inshallah! But, tell me, son. What's impossible about finding a needle in a haystack? You were lost, but now found."

The parable was deep and Escalade asked, "You speak with great knowledge, and you say the name Allah. Are you a Muslim? If so, why are you begging, and how could you ever help me?"

"I never begged you, brother. I gave you an opportunity to fulfill your deal with your Maker. I was sent as your helper. I am a builder, who was unjustly confined to my own design. When the black hair turns gray, follow the light. And your sadness is?"

"It doesn't matter. Take care," Fred said, pulling off and heading home.

When he looked into his rearview mirror, the man was gone.

****** 

Stan, D.B., One, and Two met up at the cabin. There was too much going on to hope for privacy at the office.

As D.B. filled Stan in on how Escalade's sister and girlfriend, Mia and Jazz, worked at the prison, and were the other half of a major drug ring inside, Stan was astonished. Not knowing how many correctional officers were involved and how many prisoners made up the God-body Nation was going to make matters difficult. Yet, they'd catch more bees with honey.

"But who's doing the killings?" Stan asked. "First, one of you twins killed somebody, and then the only witness gets killed. D.B., you were ahead of the pack during the first murder, but what puzzles me is the twins were with you during the second."

The twins looked at D.B. like he told Stan, and were feeling some type of way. D.B. knew he said nothing and gave them a clueless look, raising both hands to indicate that he didn't know.

Then it struck D.B., causing his heart to race. "Stan, I didn't tell you the twins shot someone, and they were with me when the witness got shot. Escalade couldn't have told anyone because I rode with him, and I didn't even know anything myself until I saw the news. So how you figure?"

"I got a call from Roger, who's on the case after the witness got killed, and whatever is going on at the prison superceded the investigation. It's being left to the locals to sort out. How Roger knew this beats the heck out of me. Where was City all the while? Because I know I know him, or we've met before recently."

"He's a one of a kind!" Two teased, of course making his brother laugh, who, after being stared at by Stan, said, "Cool, na man, everyt'ing criss!"

"Mothafucka! That's it! That's where I met him. I was coming out of my office, rushing to intercept you guys, and bumped into him outside, coming down the stairs. It was like hitting a brick wall, and when I asked him was he okay, excuse me, or something, his exact words were, 'Everyt'ing criss'! That stuck in my head because I didn't know why he thought my name was Chris!"

"So run a sheet on City. One, Two, do your CSI bullshit and match his picture off your cell phone by the retina in his eye. I'll even paint the Acura and give it back."

They both got on the case.

"Doug, find out everything about Fred, Mia, and Jazz. Pull employment records, high school and medicals. We have an issue, boys. Wait! Where's City now, and what do you think he's doing besides telling?" Stan pondered, raising good questions.

"Trying to tell," D.B. answered like he was in a race. "But if Roger is at the prison or involved with that investigation, they'd make him unavailable to City."

"Good point, Douglas. Call him, go find him, and don't let him out of your sight. Talk to Wanda and see if he had an opportunity to leave the Heights when they were together. See who she and every girl that night with y'all are. We have to see how they are built, because they could become problems."

"One and Two, call me when you find something solid. I'm going to check Wanda and friends. Any info at the prison let me know at once. From this point on, wear your vest and carry only your authorized weapons to cover our own asses. You never know!"

D.B. left, driving a black Hummer equipped with all the

latest technology. It was an office on wheels.

"Hello, Wanda? This is D.B. Are you around?"

"Kind of. What's going on?"

"I'm trying to plan a surprise for City, and if you got a minute, take this ride with me in my new Hummer so that you can give things a woman's touch. I'll make it worth your while."

"That's what I'm talkin' about! I'm at the Heights. He's been gone for over an hour. It's all good."

"I'll be there in three minutes."

"Okay, bye!"

D.B. pulled up, pressing a button, which caused the dash to transform back into a normal Hummer dash, concealing all the extra technology.

Wanda smiled to show her approval of such a beautiful piece of machinery.

"Hello, Wanda! Don't you look nice today."

"Thank you, D.B. What's the deal?"

"I just enjoyed myself so much the other night. I'm certain you two enjoyed yourselves, as well. With the business I'm in, I like to keep a tight circle. My crew is family to me, and since we all clicked, what's the best day and time to get up again? I know a little dumb shit jumped off at the club, but we didn't start that."

"I have to get back to you on the day and time because we all work, besides dancing. Some of my girls are stuck at work now, and I don't know what the hell has happened. Don't you watch the news?"

"Not really. Why, what happened?"

"San Dora's been on the news all day…lockdown."

D.B. almost hit a parked car when she said that. He swerved a bit and found a parking lot where he pulled over to get his bearings.

"So the nurses were kept there. too?" he asked.

Wanda began to laugh, because men always assumed women had to be nurses, especially in the prison system. What about C.O.'s and doctors?

"I feel ya, country," Wanda said. "Maybe in Idaho women

are only nurses or kitchen workers, but in the Tri-State, plenty of women are C.O.'s, and we're 'bout it! April's a doctor up the way, and the rest of us are correctional officers. We just live and have fun, just like men do. We all make six-figures and it doesn't bother us to be called a bitch. Just not for free. It's wanna-be niggas that think shit sweet – get it twisted. Our guns bust and we have permits."

"I hear you. Wow! It's a small world. You must know Jazz and Mia. They work there."

"You mean Fred's people? I just let him live, but I used to change his diapers. I'm eleven years his senior, and his mother and my mother are friends. Mines moved south to retire, and I had a career here and stayed. He was just a baby. He doesn't remember me. Mia just started, and Jazz been holding it down."

"So you know Fred has them selling in there?"

"He wish! I know the real deal. His sista put him on just recently. Don't say nothing, though. Come to think of it, you work for him. How does the 'help' get new Hummers and long money? 'Cause I might be in the wrong business."

"I work for Uncle Sam."

"Like hell! You don't even pay taxes on drug sales."

"I'm not really a drug dealer."

"And I'm not really a stripper."

They both laughed.

"So all your girls hustle?"

"It depends on what you consider *hustlin'*. Some sell drugs, some fuck for a buck," Wanda said.

"You seem very down to earth. Let's help each other."

"What, you want some pussy?"

'No, no! But not like that. You know what I mean, right?"

"So, what is it? Some head, or you wanna eat?"

"*No! No!* This is some serious shit. But I'll take a rain check, if I could ?"

"Well, we've been pulled over so long that you done got my panties wet for nothing. You owe me, nigga!"

"I'm about to save your life, Wanda, and you can save the

lives of your entire crew. Brace yourself for what I'm about to say."

"Don't tell me you're gay, too! I've been hearing that too much lately. Fuck the down-low!"

"My name is Special Agent Douglas Greene, and I work for the DEA. I took this job to help people, and that was part of my oath. No one protects and serves, but today we can change that."

"Stop bullshitting! You lie more than Fred. This probably a rental! Give me some dough. I gotta go."

Doug reached for his wallet and pressed a button transforming the dash to reveal his onboard futuristic accessories.

"You wasn't jokin'! That other car was bulletproof, wasn't it? Your boys killed that nigga!"

"One of your girls killed the only witness. Some of you sell drugs and some prostitute. Let's have a truce and forget the entire thing. I'll ruin this investigation and make sure not even a name is mentioned. You just make sure Keisha and Denise, along with everyone else, are on the same page."

"Why would you risk your job for us?"

"Two reasons. Reason one is no nation rises higher than its women. Reason two, there has to come a time when a black man will risk his life to protect that same black woman and child. You carried us long enough."

"That's beautiful, Doug. That's really beautiful. I'll handle my peoples. Thank you."

"So I guess I'll be taking you home now. Where to, my queen?"

"I'm at 58 South Pine Street, the big green house on the corner."

"Forget about City because he's an informant for the FBI. He just doesn't know that One, Two, and I are DEA. The two agencies never got along, so fuck 'em! If he calls, though, call me and let me know where he's at. Aren't you forgetting this?"

Reaching out to Wanda, he handed her five crisp one-hundred dollar bills.

****** 

Doug called Stan to tell him the news. Within a couple of weeks, this case had become huge. Whoever thought law and drug dealers encountered so many surprises?

"Hi, Stan. You're gonna need a seat for this. Are the twins still there? If so, put us all on speaker.

"I just left Wanda and she knows we're DEA. Peep the fly shit, though. I mean, here's something more amazing. She and all of the lovely women whom we thought was just some stripper hoes are correctional officers. She used to change Fred's diapers when he was a baby. He just didn't recognize her because it's been so long. Also, it's Mia who supplies him with the drugs, and a lot of the C.O.'s sell up the way, be it drugs or sex."

"Here's the deal, and I need everyone's cooperation on this. They forget what they saw the twins do, and we forget the entire case."

One and Two screamed, "Deal!" but Stan was the voice of reason.

"How can we turn our backs on the law?" he asked, as if no one had an answer.

"The same way our people fill up the prisons with punishment not fittin' the crime, outrageous bonds, and probation violations, whereas you have no defense. Shall I continue?" said One.

"How about St. Augustine was right when he said, 'An unjust law is no law at all. If punishment does more bad than good, then that act should be illegal, too'," said Two.

"Okay! I get your point. Well, Doug, come on in and we'll work on a plan. See you soon," Stan said.

"Okay, I'm on my way."

****** 

Wanda called who she could reach and finally got through to Jazz. They had a special code to page one another in emergencies.

"Hi, Wanda! What's up?"

"Girl, all hell has broken loose. What's good with you?"

"It's all fucked up in here. But I'm 'bout to get all this shit straight in a minute."

"Y'all on the news and everything. What happened?"

"A prisoner got shot by Becca, that new Mexican-looking bitch. Another nigga paid her, but the warden flipped over the shit, panicked, and locked shit down. Brianna done beat his ass, so I fucked him up, too, 'cause he was poppin' mad shit earlier. And Mia done kicked the nigga's dentures out his mouth. I done pulled my heat out on Lt. Larry, Leeza, and Becca. I'm getting Malik now, and Mia went to get his boy, Born, so that we can sort it all out."

"So if you're going to get Malik and Mia went to get Born, who's watching Lt. Larry, Leeza, Becca and the warden?"

"Brianna's 'bout it, chile. That bitch is the one who set it off first with the warden. She holdin' 'em down with my heat, and she ain't afraid to bust no gun. She here for some rah-rah gun-related shit."

"Well, I'm giving you one hour to call me back at this number. It's not as bad as you think. I got a new connect that can save all our asses."

"Who you got? Don't tell me Jesus done jumped off the cross!"

"Stop playing! On my word, if I don't hear from you in an hour, I'm coming in. Now, is you 'bout it?"

"All day! Holla!" Jazz said, and then hung up.

# Chapter Twenty-Two

## Brianna's Revenge

Mia went to get Born Freedom, while Jazz headed in the opposite direction to get Malik.

Brianna still had everyone at gunpoint, ignoring their pleas and small talk. Finally, it sounded as if the warden, who was left knocked out in the bathroom, was coming around.

Lt. Larry asked, "What's that noise? It sounds like someone's kicking on the door. What did you guys do with Warden Brown?"

"What do you mean 'you guys'?" Brianna snapped, full of anger by just the mention of his name. "Better yet, I'll show you what I'ma do to him! Go drag his ass outta that bathroom! Any funny shit, and you can go with him."

"Go? Where's he going?" the lieutenant asked.

That must have been one question too many, because Brianna hauled off and pistol smacked the shit outta him, knocking all the bitch out of him.

"Oh, Jesus! Don't kill me! What did I do? What did I say? I'm sorry! Lord knows I'm sorry!" Moving swiftly, he continued, "Let

129

me grab this nigga before you accidentally make that ratchet go off, okay?"

Reaching the bathroom, Lt. Larry stood in shock by the sight of a lumped-up, bloody Warden Brown. Still full of fear, though, he grabbed Brown by the ankles and dragged him out into the open.

With the gag still over his mouth, Warden Brown was trying to mumble something, and Brianna wasn't about to let the "big secret" out.

Inflamed by emotion and fueled by rage, a sofa cushion was placed firmly over his head, along with the gun barrel. Then there were three muffled shots.

Brain matter still ended up on Lt. Larry's shoes. He wouldn't realize this until he woke up. The killing was too rich for his blood, because he fainted like a real bitch!

Brianna just stood there in a daze as Leeza and Becca carefully reached out to console her. Now that was 'bout it, or very personal. The brutality coupled with the force of her actions, they didn't need to know why.

******

Mia was informing Born Freedom of everything she knew, which really was nothing. The best news was that Jazz went to get his right-hand man, Malik.

From a distance, they studied one another's approach. Mia's heart began to bang, and Malik could not believe who he saw before him.

Born greeted Malik and got no response because his trembling hands were fixed upon Mia's face, caressing gently as if to test its realness. Her tongue entered his mouth as they embraced in such a fairytale love.

Jazz and Born were thinking the exact same thing: *Say it ain't so!*

Finally, Malik spoke to Mia. "Hello. My name is Malik, and you are?"

Her startling response was, "Master Islam Allah, your Queen and Earth who is no longer without shape and void."

This surprised everyone with her knowledge of self.

"Don't tell me he's the one from the bus!" Jazz stated. "It's really 'bout to be some shit, because, Born, that new package was the shit he left on the bus with her!"

"I know," Born elaborated further. "I knew that eventually it would lead them together, because if you love someone for the purest reasons, which by nature are to love and be loved, it will always find its way."

"So all this time you never said anything, and knew you were selling your own drugs? I don't believe that shit!" Jazz retorted.

"Seeing you happy is priceless, and my need for you outweighs any riches. I am limited to material possessions, while my cup runneth over with love for you." Born's words of endearment melted Jazz's soul.

"Malik, do you care to also explain? Because I know you knew something."

"The day you brought me the package for Lt. Larry, I wasn't certain, but I kind of knew it was ours. I just couldn't make any sense of it, and just assumed my mind was playing tricks on me. However, I did use our signature cut, the silver dust flakes, which gives off a silver hue."

"Well, don't worry about your merchandise or money, because I've been saving it for our wedding and children. So, just hold me and let's figure out a way to get through this shit first. Pardon self, God-body," Mia apologized for the profanity.

Born Freedom and Jazz were pretty much speechless after all this re-uniting and shit, and there was no telling what lay on the other side of the warden's office door as they approached it.

A distraught Lt. Larry sat in a daze, staring out of the window. Brianna, Leeza, and Becca sat emotionally with teary eyes. A lifeless Warden Brown laid in a foul-smelling, bloody heap, deader than two doorknobs.

"Damn! You said Brianna was 'bout it, but shit! Now the warden's dead!" Born said.

Malik and Mia were in another world, and nothing seemed to matter at that moment.

Brianna spoke up. "Jazz, I had to push this punk motherfucka's wig back because it was some shit!"

"Chile, you ain't gotta say no more. Fuck it! The question is... *damn!* What is the question?" Jazz wondered aloud. "Oh, oh, whatever we do, we don't have much time because Wanda and my bitches coming to get us. Watch!"

Brianna said, "We have to come up with a plan, because y'all are the realest, and this is my confession..."

## Chapter Twenty-Three

### Dear Momma

Fred sat with his head down at the computer. He was trying to regain his composure so that he could e-mail his mother to inform her of the situation with Mia and Jazz being held at San Dora. Just as he began to key in his message, he heard the front door open and then close.

"Mia!" he called out. "They finally let you and Jazz..."

Cut off mid-sentence, he was astonished to see his mother standing there.

"Freddie, come give Big Momma some suga!" she said.

He ran to her like a small child, eager to absorb all the love only a mother could afford.

"Tell me what in the hell done happened. I need the truth, son, so I can help you."

"Well, something has happened at the prison where they work, and the entire place is on lockdown. It's been on the news all day, but they're not saying nothing."

"Have you spoken to her or Jasmine yet?" Big Momma asked

with attitude.

"No, ma'am, I haven't heard a thing," he said, lying through his teeth, but his polite manners were a dead giveaway.

"Now, Freddie, I told you I need the truth, and you sitting here lying like a motherfucka! Since when don't you three stay in touch? So tell me, child, before I get to swingin'! What shit y'all got into?"

"Momma, it's not what you think!" he pleaded.

"I can't think now. Shit! Oops, you done made me cuss again. Lord, have mercy! Boy, I can't think nothing until you start talking."

"Well…" he said hesitantly.

"Well! Well, my ass, Fredrick! I just know you ain't done got those girls caught up in that dope bullshit! That's why your ass looking so stupid. Here! Take my phone and call Jasmine. She'll answer my call."

"Hello, Momma?" Jazz answered, after checking her caller I.D.

"Naw, this Fred. Momma gave me her phone to call because she knew you'd recognize the number. What's going on, and are you two alright?"

"We good, but we're in some deep shit. Momma back, huh?"

"Hell yeah, and upset is not the half!"

"Well, here's some fucked-up shit. The nigga, Akbar, got killed. The warden's dead, and Snow White is missing."

"So who's running the prison?"

"You don't wanna know! Everyone thinks the warden is, but me and your sister are."

"Oh, hell no! I hope that's not the plan."

"Big Wanda said her and the crew is coming in, and she has someone that can get us out of this mess."

"Who, Jesus?"

"That's what I said, too."

"Wait a minute. You said Wanda or Big Wanda?"

"Does it make a fuckin' difference, Mr. Strip Club?"

Fred got quiet then, and you could hear Big Momma in the

background. "Wanda who? Hand me that phone, Fred!"

"Hey, who dis?"

"This is Jasmine. Hi, Momma!"

"Don't 'Momma' me! When all this shit's over, tell Mia I'ma spank both y'all asses. Now, I heard you say Wanda. Do you mean Barbara's daughter Wanda?"

"Yes, ma'am."

"What about her? She at work, too?"

"No, but she said she's coming to get us in an hour, regardless."

"Y'all done got in some shit foolin' with dat Fred, huh?"

"Not really."

"Oh yes, really. Chile, y'all on the news nationwide. I flew back from my convention, coast to coast, because I didn't hear from nan-one a y'all. I knew something wasn't right. Give me Wanda's number. I'ma call her right now to see if I can help. I know my chile standing right there looking crazy like her brother. Y'all better pray, because you may not think God is there when you need him, but my God is never late. He's always on time! Hallelujah! Ah, glory!"

Big Momma then hung up the phone and said, "Here, boy. Put my cell on the charger and bring me the house phone and my slippers. I have to give Wanda a call to see what's going on."

"Why you gonna call her and get all in it? Y'all don't need to know each other."

"That's why you in so much shit now! Think ya ass know every damn thing. Wanda is my best friend's daughter. You remember Ms. Barbara, don't you? The one that retired and moved to Arizona? Hell, Wanda used to help change your pissy diapers. Just hand me my phone. I don't even see why I'm explaining shit to your lying, retarded ass anyway!"

"Here's the phone, and I ain't retarded either!"

Dialing the number while staring Fred down because of his mumbling, she said into the receiver, "Hey, baby! Dis Wanda? Dis Big Momma. I need to see you. I'm home."

*Click!*

By the tone in her voice, Wanda knew she'd have some explaining to do. She figured now would be the perfect time to let Special Agent Douglas Greene do all the talking.

\*\*\*\*\*\*

Big Momma went to her room and sat on the bed, calling Fred to come join her. "Reach in the back of my closet and hand me my lockbox. You know, the one you've been trying to get into all your life. You never did put shit back like you found it. That's how I know you were fuckin' with it."

Removing the key from around her neck, she opened the box, revealing hundreds of letters. Also inside was a small black velvet pouch with the drawstring knotted tightly.

Clearing her throat, as if choked up on what was about to be said, she began, "Son, I bet y'all's father is worried sick about Mia and Jasmine caught up in that prison mess. He never wanted them to work there."

Fred burst out, "What are you talking about, Momma? Daddy been dead! You said he died not long after Mia was born, remember?"

Reaching inside of her pocketbook, she handed Fred his infamous Chinese bankroll and the roll of pure hundred-dollar bills.

Further in his state of confusion, Fred asked, "How did you get my money? I had just given it to a homeless man, sealing a deal I made with God."

"Haven't I always told you children that the Lord works in mysterious ways? 'Cause you know that homeless man put this roof over your head, and is your father. He told me he called you 'son' at the store, but assumed you must have taken it as an every day figure of speech due to the age difference. See, all these letters are from him to you and your sister, since y'all became teenagers. I was just so mad, hurt, and alone that he left me here with two small children and ended up in the same prison he helped to build. All these years for the sake of not wanting to tell on his so-called homeboy! I could've killed him in that courthouse when he said he didn't tell because he ain't no punk. I was so angered with him so bad, I realized your father wasn't a punk, because he was a fuckin' fool!"

"So, Momma, what did he get blamed for?"

"It supposed to been a robbery and a lot of money and jewelry wound up missing. He said he had just cashed his paycheck at the liquor store and was catching a ride home when the police tried to pull them over. It was a little chase, but with traffic being so heavy, his friend jumped out the car and got away. Mr. Not-knowing-what-the-hell-is-going-on-I-ain't-running-'cause-I-ain't-do-nothing got twenty-five years flat. Eventually, as the years passed, he constantly wrote, and one day, somehow he mailed a house key with a note. The note read: Love is a house. So actually, he gave us a better environment and a chance in life by exercising the right to remain silent."

Raising his voice a little too much, upset or not, he shouted, "So all this time you knew he was alive and lied to us and said he was dead?"

Smacking the flames out of him, Big Momma stated firmly, "Remember this, mister. I didn't lie to you. I had to respect your father's wishes. You are our child. We're not yours. We actually did what we thought was best. Hell, I had to get y'all on Social Security to take care and make ends meet. He really had to fake his death for some insurance money. Good thing back then there wasn't no computers everywhere like today!"

She continued. "Do you not listen over the years, because a part of having success is knowledge, and you're going to have to look, listen, and observe. Coming from the airport, your father told me that he told you everything in front of the store you needed to know. Remember, he called you 'son' and said he was sent as a helper, and that he was a builder confined to his own design."

"So you told him to help me, and what he meant was because he just got out and helped build San Dora, he could get them out, too?"

"Absolutely! I been tellin y'all children for how many years now that God is always on time."

"I don't know what to say, Momma. Can I cuss?"

"Go ahead, baby. You'sre a man."

"Damn!" Fred said.

"I know you can do better than that. I done heard you, Jasmine, and your sista out back cussing up a storm, thinking I'm sleep and can't hear y'all."

With a tear falling down her face, she showed Fred the last family photo the four of them took together that she kept in her pocketbook.

"Let me get myself together, 'cause he'll be here in a minute…"

# Chapter Twenty-Four

**Control**

It was a little past lunchtime when the prisoners began getting restless and hungry. The dorms especially were beginning to get out of control, and the warden's phone practically rang off the hook.

Many National Guardsmen were posted outside of the gates, armed on standby. Little did they know, the countdown had already begun for Mr. AWS, the highly classified government investigation breach alert. Now remember, the gang days of Connecticut were long gone and the guards controlled that system. However, in New Jersey, the Muslims ran the bing.

Born Freedom placed Born C, Tone, and Smitty in charge of the cellblocks. The Sunni brothers sent their Sutra team to the dorms to maintain order. Old School was rolling tough and smacked a white guard off gates to prove shit was real, and locked him in a cell for a change.

Old School used to be a thug, but now he just drank a lot, and that's about it. He had larceny in his heart and took the guard's wallet, pack of cigarettes, and began singing on his walkie-talkie, "Two whole beef patties, special sauce, lettuce, cheese, tomato, onion…" just fucking up the Big Mac song, as he headed for the kitchen. He grabbed five hardworking Mexicans and a couple of punks, stating, "We 'bout to really get it cookin' in here. Lunch will soon be served!"

After delegating everyone an assignment, the smell of fried onions and burgers gave the men something to look forward to. With their stomachs growling, they decided to save their energy and kick back and wait, because Old School understood their need for pacification.

Announcing over the intercom that today's lunch was "All you can eat, or until I get tired of cooking" brought humor to the situation.

But still…was there a plan?

# Chapter Twenty-Five

## Confessions

When the black Hummer pulled in behind Fred's Escalade, he didn't know who to expect. Once Wanda hopped out from behind the limo tint, there was some relief. Yet, when D.B. emerged from behind the wheel wearing a gold jersey with red letters reading DEA on it, Fred almost had a heart attack.

All sorts of thoughts were running through his head. He was about to run, but couldn't leave his mother in such an awkward position.

D.B.'s 9mm was holstered at his waist, along with a shiny gold badge and chrome handcuffs dangling from the rear.

Wanda spoke. "Don't worry; he's down with us. Hey, Momma, this is our blessing in disguise; indeed, he is. This is Special Agent Douglas Greene of the DEA. This is Big Momma to all, Fred and Mia's mother."

"Pleased to meet you, I think. Wanda, how you gonna bring the police to my home at a time like this? You know these chil'ren don got into a whole bunch of shit now. Half my life I've waited for my husband to come on out from behind those bars, and now my chil'ren. I need a drank! Fred, go in your stash in my freezer and bring me that bottle of Henny you keep behind the frozen greens, like nobody knows. And quit lookin' so damn scary. Ain't nobody stud'n you. If Wanda said that he is down with us, and he ain't grab you yet, 'cause I know you the ringleader, hell, let him talk to see what's the deal. Go on, baby."

"How are you, ma'am, or may I call you Big Momma, please?"

"No, please, just Big Momma if you mean right by my kids."

"This may get kind of confusing, but don't worry yourself with the fine details. You see, I work for your son here, Escalade, while he and Jazz work for your daughter, Mia."

"Oh, naw! Not my baby! There has to be a mistake. Fred, hurry up with my drank, and I know good and well you ain't got folks calling you 'Escalade'! See, you and that motherfuckin' truck gonna be sitting right in a cell together!"

"Really, Big Momma, a lot has happened in the last couple of weeks. Things like multiple murders, drug dealing, and prison corruption. My thing is my agents went out of bounds and committed themselves to criminal activity. I must admit, I, too, dabbled myself on the wild side of the law. The bottom line is it's now a Black thing, and together, we can make all of this disappear and remain the best of friends with lucrative standings."

Fred disagreed quickly. "Yeah, right! You played me! I can handle my time 'cause I ain't kill nobody."

Cutting her eyes to Fred, Big Momma gave him that "shut the fuck up" look that he knew very well.

Special Agent Greene explained, "Fred, I'm a brotha first and agent second. If I can't decide to help my own people and myself, it would be foolish of me to exist. Nothing ever goes as planned for us, and we're never under normal circumstances in America. Whether it is me or you, do you think the government gives a fuck who they lock up next? Since you're so smart, did you realize that conspiracy to commit a crime can get you the full sentence…even life? Hear me good. There doesn't even have to be a likelihood that you actually could pull off such a crime. Just talking about it or knowing of it gives you more than any of us can handle, unless you feel as though you can muster up nine lives, because kilos and murders equal life imprisonment, easily!"

"He's fine with your plan, Dougie," Big Momma agreed for him.

"That's 'Douglas', Big Momma!"

"Look! I said 'Dougie' and this is my house! Who your people anyway? You kind of favor ole water head Stan and Walt Greene, bless the dead. You know, they messed 'round, I heard, with the same woman, but you ain't heard it from me."

"Well, I see where Fred gets his sense of humor from," D.B. laughed.

Just as D.B. was about to explain in detail some sort of plan, another car pulled up. It was a white Cadillac Deville with limo tint, sitting on some barely legals (18-inch rims). The horn blew the same rhythmic pattern of some two decades ago.

Immediately recognizing his signature tootin', Big Momma ran to the bay window and waved for him to come inside.

He exited the car, not looking homeless at all. His silk shirt was partially unbuttoned, revealing his muscular physique and heavy gold herringbone chain. The swagger must have been genetic, because he walked in a "Z" formation; like father, like son! Accenting such a first impression sparkled a very modest three-karat pinky ring.

"Well, I see we're having a party and have a special guest," he said, referring to Special Agent Douglas Greene because of the DEA shirt, gun, and badge. "I'll be right back. I left my headlights on," and went to about face when Big Momma stopped him.

"Herman, quit acting so crazy. Don't you have daytime running lights? This here is a friend of ours, and I bet you don't know who she is," Big Momma said, pointing to Wanda.

"Ruby, who don't? That's Barbara's chile – my godchild. Look just like her momma, much as she used to charge to change Fred's doo-doo diapers. Wasn't no Pull-ups then. It was more like rinse-offs. Remember she use to hold his little butt up to the faucet and rinse it clean?

"This here police look familiar, too. Look like ole water head n'em. What's your people name? Gotta be dem water head Greene's or those long head Johnsons, 'cause they all had them heads."

"I'm Special Agent Douglas Greene, sir. And you are?"

"Boy! You look just like your people. Look at him, Rube! Don't he look just like dem Greene's? Ole long jug heads. I know you *keep* a headache! Sorry to hear about Walt and Mary passing. They was my folks. Excuse the stutter. I got excited. Me and Stan go way back, at least twenty-five years flat."

Big Momma interrupted fast before Herman got started about how Stan Greene left him to take the weight for a crime he committed. He did end up giving him half the money and jewels, but they hadn't faced one another since to peace it up.

Big Momma skillfully agreed with her husband by saying, "Yeah, he do look like his folks. Now, can we get on with a plan, because my babies are up in there, and all types of things could be happening?"

******

"Soon all of this mess will be over," Brianna said. "We have about four hours or so to go."

Born asked, "Why do you say four hours or so, as if you know something we don't?"

"Exactly. So, we might as well get on the same page."

"And?" Born Freedom said defensively and full of sarcasm, while everyone else's ears were attuned. "It can't get no worse. What you, da police?"

Standing out of reach with gun still in hand, Brianna answered with his natural manly voice. "Exactly! I'm Detective Brian St. John."

Everybody stood in disbelief and with blank stares upon their faces. No one could find words to combat this revelation.

"Please, let me explain, because we need each other to get out of this shit," Brian said, not too convincingly.

Mia finally spoke up. "Are you the police for real? Since when do they got undercovers in prison with titties and fat asses? This is some bullshit! I hustle in jail and still get caught. Somebody pinch me and tell me I'm fuckin' dreaming!"

Jazz was really at a loss for words and felt betrayed, because for over a year, she and Brianna became close. They exchanged sexual encounters, makeup tips, and even tampons, let alone got money together.

"How can you be the police? You've been in here for over a year, living just like every other prisoner. You're too feminine to be a police. You just talking reckless because it's a lot going on right now and you're losing it, still with my gun in your hand. Police do not kill unarmed wardens," Jazz figured.

"That was personal and a reason why I said we need each other to get out of this shit. I've always heard y'all refer to who's 'bout it and who ain't, and you guys showed me a lot of love. I was planted here to investigate allegations of the warden having sex with prisoners, and stumbled across your drug ring. The State made me stay in here longer to try and find out more dirt on everyone. But once I got attached to you, Jazz, and the type of money we were getting, I began fuckin' that case all up. I told them I wanted to go home, but they didn't give a fuck about me. So, once the warden tried to push up on me and take my shit, I had to give it to him. What is it? This gun in my hand makes you think I'm your enemy now? Ain't no need to be the police now. I'm 'bout it!"

*Pop! Pop!* Two bodies hit the floor.

Becca and Lt. Larry died instantly, one shot apiece to the head. No one wanted to speak because it may have triggered another fatality.

Brian realized the loss for words, but no longer could sense tension between them, nor disbelief in his position. "I killed them because they would end up having all of us doing life. Becca told quickly that Malik paid her fifty G's to kill Akbar and that Lt. Larry was the one that introduced them. Then Lt. Larry let the bitch come out of him, afraid of just the sight of blood. I couldn't chance that, feel me?"

"Hell yeah!" they said in unison. "You either crazy than a motherfucka or 'bout it!"

"I must be crazy…done killed three people in one day. Then again, the State left me locked up for over a year. Fuckin' with y'all, shit, I'm 'bout it—'bout it! That little change my job paid me for all this shit is nothing compared to what we made and I done stole for us. My momma ain't raise no fool. Jazz, take this hot-ass gun with no serial numbers."

"Hey, that was a good thing, fuckin' with you. What about this money, and how we gonna get up out this shit?" Jazz asked. "Shit! Wanda, Denise, Keisha, and China are on their way. How they getting in beats the hell outta me!"

Malik finally had something to say. "Yo, you dead-ass about being 'bout it, huh? You really been clappin' shit up. Shit, you ain't got no choice but to be 'bout it," he said, exchanging a manly embrace of acceptance.

Born agreed. "Yea, fam, you hood with yours. So what's the plan, though?"

"Well, everybody done ate except us. Let's make sure everybody is away from the kitchen, because we need to dispose of the bodies, and torching this office would be the easiest way to get rid of any evidence, including DNA, fibers, and any other CSI bullshit."

"Why the kitchen?" Leeza asked, finally speaking.

"We're going to cook the bodies, then grind them up, and flush them out to sea. No one would expect that, and the fish will eat all the evidence. Then we let a few people wild out while setting a few fires, and then make a few white guards heroes. Trust, they'll go right along with the program. It's their nature. Hell, they were in Hollywood and said it was the moon, remember?

"I'm bringing charges against the warden and say he snuck out somehow and is at large with Akbar. We just have to find Snow White before everything hits the fan, and if she ain't dead, she gotta go. That bitch is too emotional."

****** ******

Herman revealed to everyone that every major State facility throughout the entire country always has an emergency exit. Being that he helped build San Dora, there was no need to rely on a blueprint. These types of routes were never inked in on floor plans. Luckily, he knew exactly the mighty fortress's only weaknesses.

The twins arrived with heavy firepower, just when Denise, Keisha, China, and April appeared out of nowhere, wearing all-black fatigues and bandanas. There was no small talk, no smiles, and no formal introductions. These women were trained assassins. The only question remaining was...where's City?

Herman said, "Describe him," while the rest of them seemed irritated, as if that was an irrelevant question at this point in time.

"Dad, you don't know him, so let's go!" Fred said.

Frozen back in time, Big Momma shouted joyously, "Hallelujah!" as Herman shed a single tear. Fred called him "Dad", making him speechless with only enough strength to point to his trunk. Using his remote keyless entry, he popped it open, disclosing City, who was gagged and hog-tied.

"Well, I remember you told me he couldn't swim," Wanda said. "So, let's feed him to the fishes on the way."

"That's a plan. Let's move out and we'll go over any other details at the point of entry," D.B. commanded.

"Good luck, y'all, and bring my babies home!" Big Momma waved.

# Chapter Twenty-Six

## Not Missing a Beat

Stan had to stay one step ahead of D.B. a.k.a. Special Agent Greene and the twins. Little did they know, even their vests had GPS devices on them. Plus, they were wired for sound and didn't have a clue.

There was so much going on that he was overwhelmed by how a routine drug sting turned out to all hell breaking loose.

After reaching Special Agent Roger Hawkins, they agreed to meet and exchange information involving the gas station murder and strip club homicide. Roger figured his place because he had unfinished business with his prisoner, Snow White, to tend to.

Stan was mentally prepared to do whatever it took to protect Douglas and the twins. He figured they had come too far to let one white man turn them around. Their reasoning earlier was quite convincing, after all.

Being buzzed in at the electronic gate, Roger waited at the door, drink in hand. "Hello, home skillet! Welcome to my crib," he laughed. "If I knew you were coming, I would have barbecued some pork, fried some chicken, or made grape Kool-Aid!"

"Fuck you, you air-guitar, fake Don Johnson, 'Miami Vice'-looking bitch! By the way, My said to tell you 'hi'."

"My, who?" Roger asked.

"My dick! You barefoot hillbilly! Where's my drink?"

"Do I look like 'Benson'? No offense. I'm not prejudice. Hell, you're not the only colored person I have over. Somebody has to clean up," Roger chuckled, pouring Stan a double Hen' on the rocks.

"Can we get down to business now? Because I'm sure you don't want to miss 'Hee Haw' on TV later."

"Sure, no problem." Roger pulled out a clear picture of one of the twins and a clear marker plate of the alleged shooter's vehicle at the gas station. "The intersection camera took a motion picture of someone exiting the car, running one way, and seconds later, back, just when smoke and flames could be seen from everywhere."

"That's nothing," Stan said, trying to shrug it off.

"You know your people are nosey and would have stayed around to watch. And why the hoody overhead? It wasn't cold outside. Dude looked like a lady, too, because I can see nail polish with some sort of design on those fingernails. What's baffling me is the plate belongs to a female correctional officer. And guess where she works?"

"Don't say San Dora, 'cause it's a lot of that going around."

"What do you mean?"

"Well, you had company, didn't you? And they left behind their DOC jacket hanging on the back of your chair. I know you were freaky, but sugar in the tank? Dude, I didn't know you were on the down-low. So what's his name? Big Bubba?"

"Have a drink. You're gonna need it."

"Wanna get laid right now?"

"Look, man. I don't go that route. No thanks!"

"Not me, stupid. I got a bitch hostage in my bedroom role-playing. She's into body worship and bondage, so I got her cuffed and gagged."

"Let me see, Rog. I ain't had no white bitches in a minute."

"Alright, but ain't no trying to get to know her or slip her your number for later type of shit. Just stick your head in the door and let me know."

Peeking in the bedroom, Stan excitedly confirmed, "Oh, yeah, she's a fox. Roger, where you kidnap her from?"

"Actually, she came to me through a good friend and business associate of mine."

"I'll have a crack at that, if you don't mind. No videotaping or kinky shit either. Plus, once I pull my shit out, the whole room will get dark!"

"Okay, 'Moby Dick'. You just remember; who's the man?"

"Oh, you definitely the man! I'll be back," he said, imitating Schwartzeneger in *The Terminator*.

Stan went into the room, stripped down naked, and approached the woman flinching on the bed. He turned the nightstand radio/alarm clock on, catching a slow jam station, as if setting the mood. However, he was really trying to create noise distortion – knowing how Roger gets down – so that he could whisper in her ear.

"Don't worry. I know who you are and I'm going to get you out of here. Just go along with the program and I'll leave you with my handcuff key and extra firearm for you to handle shit. Trust me. I know everything, and you'll walk away minus a scratch."

As they continued to rub bodies, Stan couldn't resist any longer. His dick was hard as hell, and Snow White's pussy was soaked from him sucking on her nipples. He grunted, putting his dick in her raw. "We got to make it look real good in case he's watching us. I'll make it good…I mean quick!"

Stan was pounding on her hot, wet pussy, definitely enjoying this part of the investigation. Since he had a little freak in him, he ate the pussy, too! He was just a licking and a sucking the clit, legs, ankles, ass and toes on this white bitch. Shit! Who could blame him, though? Snow White was the type that reminded you of Ice T's wife, Coco. But ain't this some shit! Once he got that nut, he had a change of plans. Stan wanted to keep the pussy and kill

Roger his damn self.

So, he whispered in her ear, "Give me two hours to make sure everything goes according to plan, and I'll be right back for you."

Just like a man thinking with a dick

Wiping his sweat, and leaving DNA everywhere and not giving a fuck, Stan felt good.

So good that he came out of the room and told Roger, "Yeah, my nigga, that was some good shit! How about another—" then he quickly grabbed Roger with some two-finger, Mr. Spock, Vulcan grip-type shit. Roger's tipsy ass was out cold in an instant. Hand-to-hand-combat-Stan was always swift with pressure points and shit. Plus, Roger's drinking made it that much easier.

Stan ran a tub of water and let Roger's unconscious body soak, washing away any evidence off of him, while setting the atmosphere for a perfect suicide. Putting a silencer on Rogers service weapon and placing it in his left hand, they squeezed together, sending brain upon the tiles. The hot barrel even left a burnt mark to make it more convincing.

Rifling through his files, Stan discovered just what he needed to link Warden Brown and Roger together. There was a ledger of many transfers and a list of deceased former prisoners with very similar descriptions, who had filed grievances regarding the warden's conduct and sexual advances toward them. With all of that going on at San Dora, there was now a perfect motive for suicide.

Stan double-checked the scene and left to meet up with everyone else in route to San Dora. His plan was still to come back for round two, seeing as that was more important to him than the person.

# Chapter Twenty-Seven

### The Point of No Return

Three vehicles deep, they headed for San Dora. At the bridge, D.B. turned on his flashing lights, bringing traffic to a distant halt. The twins went quickly to the trunk of the Deville, zapped City with a stun gun, untied him, and tossed him over to swim with the fishes.

Reaching the nearby park, a hidden sewer manhole was actually a well undisclosed entrance to the secret tunnel leading to San Dora. After clearing the brush, they engaged to enter.

Wanda placed a text message to Jazz by just a numeric code, signaling their arrival.

Their plan was simple: in and out, pardon the pun, but taking no prisoners. All you could hear were weapons being cocked, promising one in the chamber.

******

The make-believe riot began, just as the cooking, grinding, and flushing was underway. Good thing San Dora still had the old plumbing with no built-in traps. Everyone knew just to make it look good and not seriously injure any guards. There was no way anyone would dare question why. Tone, Smitty, and Old School had everything under control.

Since the little white dude from earlier was in for arson, he volunteered to burn down the warden's office. Then, he and Born C tore up the kitchen, causing an explosion that wreaked havoc.

There was no more standby. The State Police and Reserve National Guard began marching into the gate. Then, suddenly, an entourage of black Suburban's pulled up, with Governor Gary Nulls, along with his personal tactical squad, inside.

Bullhorn in hand, the New Jersey governor ordered, "Stand down, troopers! Stand down!" Meanwhile, his force was silent, in single file, and ready for whatever. He was getting suited up, as well, because he was going in!

The news cameras were turned on their every move. Every station began buzzing again with breaking news.

At home, worried sick, Big Momma sat glued to the TV.

"Breaking news! This is Shamik Shatanae reporting live from San Dora. There has been an awful explosion of some sort, causing National Guards and troopers to finally enter what looks like the beginning of a war zone. However, if you look to my right, you'll see that Governor Nulls and his elite squad have taken over, pulling everyone else back outside to the perimeter. Yes, the governor himself has suited up and armed himself, ordering everyone else to stand down. There must be one of their own inside for him to be taking the matter personal. Shekeem Harold, back to you in the studio."

"Thank you, Shamik. There you have it. Whatever it is, it's going down! You can see the smoke-filled chaos at hand. We'll keep you informed of any new developments. For now, this has been Shekeem Harold, reporting from our satellite office, bringing you the 411 at Channel 77 News."

******

In no time, Herman led everyone through the underground tunnel. It was nothing fancy, just off-white painted concrete and dimly lit wall lighting. They ended up right outside of the warden's office window, formerly marked "Emergency Exit", which was also the only unbarred window in the entire facility. The bushes were just far enough away from the building to act as a shield, giving standing room for two at a time only.

Using her D.O.C. radio, Wanda called for Jazz and Mia to regain control and state their location.

Mia signaled back, over all the noise, "Where are you?"

Wanda, being all dramatic in her *Mission Impossible* mode, said, "In Brown Bear's den," evidently meaning the warden's charred office.

That's when D.B. said into the walkie-talkie, "This is Special Agent Douglas Greene of the DEA. Meet us in Brown Bear's den at once! We have more unexpected guests with heavy firepower heading your way."

"Roger that! This is Detective Brian St. John of the New Jersey State Police Deep Cover Defense Unit. We're on our way."

The marching and chanting was getting closer and closer. The sound of the bullhorn became frightening. All you could hear was, "Allah u Akbar-*Stomp!* Allah u Akbar-*Stomp!* Muhammad ar Rasulallah-*Stomp!*" You could no longer see their faces and their enormity was terrifying. The smallest of them had to be 6'6" and 305 pounds solid.

The prison got under control in record-breaking time, and those officers selected to become heroes cooperated just as planned. Of course, a few inmates would get pardons, especially if Detective St. John had his way.

Once reaching the tiny corridor, which led to the warden's office, Fred screamed with joy, happy to see Mia and Jazz approaching. All of the other ladies gave their special handshakes and hugged.

Malik and Born both embraced Herman, which surprised everyone. They greeted him with, "Peace, God Supreme!"

"Peace, my sons. Yes, it is peace," he responded.

Fred said to Mia, "Look! This is our father!" referring to Herman, who had up the way changed his name to God Supreme to hide his old identity. "Don't I look just like him?" he asked, flexing his chest and bragging.

"Wow!" Malik and Born Freedom said.

Mia was speechless and had to really take a good look at them.

*They do resemble*, she thought.

All the while, Detective St. John and Special Agent Greene had introduced themselves, and agreed to a simple plan to be most affective. Gathering everyone's attention, it went like this:

"None of the girls were at work today. All of the time clocks are electronic and computerized, and St. John has taken care of the entire system, permanently," Agent Greene said. "As for the rest, they're all at large as far as our reports will read once the smoke clears.

"Born Freedom and Malik, go with Detective St. John and he'll take care of you guys, because his people should be making their way inside by now."

"I feel an early retirement coming on. Who's with me?" St. John asked everyone, hinting that they were all about to be paid in full.

Wasting no more time, they all went on their way just as planned.

******

The few guards were bought and paid for by fame and glory. Their philosophy was order had to be restored with the public's safety in mind first and foremost. They agreed – *wink-wink!*

Detective Brian St. John stood front and center with a blanket wrapped around him, not wanting the world to see he had breasts.

Governor Nulls saluted him and said, "This deserves a promotion, soldier!"

"I doubt it. Once the smoke clears, we both need to quit this shit!" Brian said with a wink. "I just have to make sure these fine gentlemen get their just due for helping, and that these brave correctional officers get promoted after a month's paid vacation or something. You think?"

"Not a problem," the governor assured him.

"I'll have my full report on your desk in a week, sir. I need to take these guys into custody now, and come back tomorrow for a couple more who deserve your pardon, as well."

"Whatever you think is fair," the governor saluted, as Brian, Born, and Malik headed for the front door.

Looking back, St. John asked, "What? Are we supposed to walk? And by the way, we need some cash for Burger King! Don't we, fellas?"

# Chapter Twenty-Eight

**Finally!**

Everyone had gathered at Big Momma's for a little celebrating, although it wasn't over quite yet. There was plenty of food and drink to accompany such a festive mood.

Mia excused herself and went to freshen up and gather her thoughts. After a nice hot shower, she laid quietly, thinking about Malik, who, to her surprise, was on his way. She blocked out all the long-lost father business.

******

Meanwhile, Stan tricked Snow White out of one more round of pussy. This time, he took the gag out of her mouth and got some concentration, telling her that Roger was probably looking, because the first time was kind of quick. Apparently, he couldn't get enough, and if you saw her, you wouldn't blame him. For a white bitch, she was the truth!

Finally uncuffing her, she stormed out of the bedroom butt-naked, and ignoring the fact that Roger was already dead, she picked up his gun and emptied the entire clip into his back and head, not shedding a tear.

******

Pulling up to the drive-thru, Malik and Born Freedom ordered a double order of fish sandwiches with fries and orange sodas. Brian was torn between the Big Mac and Quarter-Pounder, causing a good laugh, because they were at Burger King, not Mickey D's.

******

Mia imagined what making love to Malik would be like, savoring their first kiss. Sleeping in the nude, the fresh-scented candle was definitely an added turn on. She began caressing her breasts slowly, with her legs spread-eagle on top of the covers. She licked her lips…

# Chapter Twenty-Nine

## Dozing Off

"Good evening! Or should I mock San Dora's protocol and say, 'Count time!'

"Mayhem alone cannot begin to describe what went on today at the prison.

"Rumor has it—and you ain't heard it from me, okay?—that New Jersey's governor, Gary Nulls, and his personal elite tactical squad did, in fact, enter the prison to rescue one of their own! When the smoke clears, we shall somehow find out who and what really happened?.

"Let's go live to the scene. Standing by, we have Shamik Shatanae, and this has been Shekeem Harold reporting from our studio, Channel 77 News."

"Thank you, Shekeem. Here you have it, what looks like a scene of a war zone. Police, fire, and paramedics are still scrambling everywhere trying to regain order and verify some type of a head count."

An explosion earlier rocked the charred, whitewashed concrete walls of the eastern corner, which I've been told is the kitchen area.

"A perimeter has been set up, and the entire city is on lockdown. The biggest fear faced evidently would be how many prisoners have escaped?

"What I will tell you, though, is that three unidentified men were escorted out of the rubble, departing in one of the governor's Suburbans. They were wearing prison tans and had their heads covered with blankets to shield their identities. We can safely assume, and based on the governor's iced-out smile, their mission has been accomplished.

"Let's try to get a word in," Shamik said, rushing towards the governor. "Excuse me, Governor Nulls! Could you tell us what went on today, and what made the matter so personal whereas you physically involved yourself?"

"It's still pure chaos and too early to predict what the real deal is. True indeed, though, we did have a few of our own planted inside the prison for quite some time now, conducting an intensive investigation."

"Was the warden involved in any way, shape, or form? And where is he now for comment?"

"Shamik, that's a good damn question! He's definitely a man of interest at the moment."

"Is he a missing piece of the puzzle, sir? I must ask because the people need to know. Will he be facing any criminal charges?"

"Call it what you want, because you know I keep it one-hundred.real !

"Governor!" Shamik warned. "We're on live TV, sir!"

"Sorry, but I'm mad as hell! He has F'd up my prison and he owes me 'twenty' damn dollars! See, he done let this governor title and suits fool his ass. He better recognize! These hands work! Knockout! Turn out!"

"So you're saying it was corruption going on behind these walls and Warden Brown was involved, or at least had knowledge of it?"

"Phil! Point the damn camera over here and zoom in some. Shit!" instructed the governor to the cameraman. "I'll tell you what, Shamik, I'm exhausted and need some rest. What I will do is, because you're my favorite news station, I'm placing an official gag order on the matter and I'll give you an afternoon exclusive tomorrow."

Governor Nulls added, walking up to the camera and talking so close to it he spit on the lens, "Warden Brown, if you're out there tuned in, *better have my money! Peace!*" and turn yourself in!

As the governor walked away, talking and laughing with his entourage, he said, "I bet they didn't beep that out!"

"Thank you, sir," Shamik happily replied. "Well, enough said for tonight. We'll be in suspense until *mañana*. I'm Shamik Shatanae, reporting live from San Dora, and looking forward to bringing you the afternoon exclusive. Shekeem, back to you in the studio, and to all a good night."

"Great job, Shamik, with landing our first ever exclusive. I bet we get some advertisers now besides the dollar store, liquor store, after-hours, and Newport. Who ever said it doesn't pay to have family in politics?" Shekeem congratulated.

"You already know what it's gonna be. I'm bettin' sex, drugs, and murder. With the entire city on lockdown, Uncle Nulls is flippin' over that 'twenty' dollars more than anything else. It's never the amount, he says, it's the principle. See, he keeps it real too, because since we're Channel 77 News, why do you think he's giving us an afternoon exclusive?" Shekeem asked no one in particular.

"You know we're not getting up at no five and six o'clock in the morning worrying about some news. If shit happen that early, it's none of our damn business, feel me?

"Again, this has been Shekeem Harold, reporting. Shout out to Ren-a-sin-a! I told you, 'I ain't paying you country boys nuffin'—nuffin'!'" he sang the words.

"Channel 77 News. I'm out!"

******

After the news went off, everyone continued to celebrate and mingle. Big Momma figured the less she knew as far as the details, the better off she'd be. She thought Mia must've been too tired or overwhelmed and just called it a night, going off to bed and not even watching the news.

Everyone hoped and just knew it had to have been Brianna, Malik, and Born Freedom who left San Dora with the blankets over their heads. That would be a lovely surprise for Mia, since she's the only one that didn't watch the news with everyone else.

*Calling Brianna "Detective Brian St. John" was going to take some getting used to,* Jazz thought. Being nasty as usual, she looked forward to really puttin' it on Born, off rip! Although Fred was there, she was really torn between the two.

Herman a.k.a. Born God Supreme, Mia and Fred's long lost father, was feeling some type of way regarding his wife, Ruby a.k.a. Big Momma. It had been quite some time since they made love. He always got excited by the smell of her Avon, and she couldn't resist his Old Spice.

Fred and Special Agent Douglas Greene—or I should say Escalade and D.B.—put their differences to the side, not wanting to let all this pussy in the room go to waste.

There were Denise and Keisha (who the twins, One and Two, thought had some of the best pussy in the world), both young... sexy... and freaks!

Then you had China, with her Oriental flavor. She was already tipsy in Fred's lap, grinding on his dick as if they were alone.

D.B. admired Wanda's oversized sensations and wondered how he could get some of that without offending April, who he had already dealt with before and wasn't done.

*Jazz and Leeza, now that would be a show!* Escalade and D.B both thought to themselves. It was just a matter of time. Once the last half-gallon of Henny was done, it would be poppin'!"

******

Right after Brian, Malik, and Born left Burger King, the trio headed to 72 Mill Street, a safe house, so Brian could immediately begin reverse treatment. Very soon, there'd be no more Brianna's cleavage. Injecting testosterone and other male hormones caused his breasts to shrink, his voice to deepen, and facial hair to grow back, along with returning his male genitalia to its original size and potency.

Brian let Malik and Born dip the Suburban, also giving them the phone number to the safe house in the event of an emergency.

Malik figured it was too late to go see his son and sort of wasn't prepared nor in the mood to deal with the baby-momma-drama. However, they both needed a change of clothes, heat (weapon), and cash. He took his bachelor pad—or honeycomb hideout—as a loss. Yet, he appreciated that the landlord always placed his belongings in storage. This had become a routine for the two.

Quietly, they arrived unannounced, just as well as unexpected. Using the spare key always left outside under the flowerpot, they tipped in. Relieved to find the alarm code still his date of birth, they let out a double sigh of relief to also find no one home.

They quickly dressed. Born Freedom was a bit overwhelmed

as to what to choose from because throwback jerseys weren't out before he went in. He had a time figuring out what to wear. After all that time of trying to decide, he settled for blue jeans and a white tee.

While all of this was going on, Malik was deep in thought, writing a note to leave behind. He always tried to be considerate to her because she was more than just his baby's momma. Ever since they met, he'd had his own pet name for her.

Dear Precious:

Although we're not together, why are we so far apart? It's late, and I'm assuming that you've been watching the news, as usual. Therefore, I already know you and my little man are at your mother's house. I just came to change my clothes because I have a few moves to make by morning.

I already know I've got some explaining to do, and you'll get your chance once again to say, "I told you so!"

It's all good, though, and the price you pay when you "spin the wheel"!

I got Born Freedom with me, too, so I'll see you tomorrow.

Love,
Malik

P.S. Born's been walking on your carpet with his shoes on and he's been in your kitchen! He said holla back!

Just before leaving, Malik went to the hidden wall safe and grabbed two "ninas" (9mm) because everything is real in the "murda field" (streets). He also grabbed two stacks of cash, five-thousand apiece, just enough to get a nun naked if she had to.

Really though, they had plenty of cash to parlay with for one night. Of course, they were horny, and sex was the only thing on the agenda.

They figured it would be best to take two vehicles just in case they split up later. So, Malik pulled out his 2000 CLK 430 coupe, and let Born push the big boy truck. Not the Suburban, but the BMW M5, which drove much better. Plus, the Suburban had State plates that read "GOV-2" on them. Not a good thing late night in the hood.

Born Freedom was excited by the look of the chrome 22's, TV's in the dash, headrests, and ceiling, and the I-Pod system. The butterscotch leather with the metallic flake candy-green paint were his favorite colors, too.

Malik said, "Yo, God, we'll leave the 'burb in the driveway and you can follow me to Mia's, because that's probably where everybody's at. I'm in the coupe and you need to see how you like your whip. Welcome home, fam!"

"Say word, this is mine? I need a whip, too, and it's my color. Hell yeah! This bi-otch got everything I wanted. This shit only got thirty-three miles on it," he said from behind the wheel. "How come?"

"'Cause it's yours. I bought it for you and got it done up just the way you always talked about on the phone. This was the last year for this body style, so I was just sittin' on it for you. Wipe them tears from your eyes and let's go get it on. It's all love!" Malik assured him, walking to his car.

"I'm good, God! I'm good," Born said after gathering himself. "Lead the way!"

******

The lights were on inside of the house and several cars were parked alongside the street. For some strange reason, the driveway was empty, as if somebody must have recently left.

As they pulled in, Jazz noticed their headlights and nudged Wanda to check and see who it could be. She crept out of the back door, alongside of the house, well within the shadows, gun in hand.

165

Malik and Born Freedom were steady talking and walking toward the house. To Wanda's surprise, they actually heard someone's presence because of the faint sound of a twig snapping. All three at the same time drew their weapons—two infrared beams against one.

From the pinch of light coming from the kitchen door that was left ajar, they were able to luckily recognize each other.

Pleased to see how handsome they were out of a prison environment, Wanda became slightly aroused. With lust in her eyes and liquor on her breath, she gave them both a big hug, allowing her free hand to cop a cheap feel.

Invitingly, she whispered, "Let's cum inside—I mean go inside—and surprise everyone."

Following her lead, Malik's first question was, "Where's Mia?"

Wanda responded, "Probably laying down in her room thinking about you."

"Show me so that I may join her!" he pleaded.

Jazz's glass and chin shattered as they both dropped to the floor, as if her eyes were deceiving her.

The sound of breaking glass got everyone's attention, except for Malik who just waved without emotion while following Wanda's pointed finger down the hallway in search of Mia.

Since Fred was already tipsy and had China all in his lap for the past half hour, it would be easy for Jazz and Born Freedom to slip away unnoticed. Not that she thought it mattered, because if she played her cards right, she'd have her cake and be eaten by two!

******

Malik tipped quietly and placed an ear to the door. His heart dropped immediately when he heard soft moans coming from inside the bedroom.

Infuriating the situation further, he heard Mia's voice saying, "Oh, yes! Fuck me, baby! Take this pussy, daddy! It's all yours... *Malik!*"

Losing it, he double-checked his nine to make sure one was in the chamber. He peeped through the keyhole, and in the dim light of the threshold, she was found all alone.

Malik could hardly pull his eye away from the keyhole. His dick was brick hard and they both wanted in. Picking the lock was a small thing, and in no time, he stood naked before her with the physique of a true and living god.

Mia was startled, shocked, and slightly embarrassed. But horny outweighed them all; that is all due to the sight before her and the continuous buzz deep inside her.

She reached for him, pulled him to her bedside, and placed his thickness inside her juicy, full lips, pumping him with one hand and her toy with the other. She sucked and licked balls and all. Her technique sent Malik straight up on his tiptoes.

Her fur bedspread was sticky and somewhat matted down by the lava flowing from her sexual volcano erupting nonstop and saturating her sugar walls.

Malik longed for just a taste because sucking on her drenched fingers was not enough. He double-checked to make sure the door was locked and hung his shirt over the knob so that it draped down over the keyhole. One would think there was about to be some heavy traffic and a brother didn't want to get caught "going downtown".

Strategically, he guided her onto her flat stomach, gripping her tight ass cheeks firmly. He then placed hot, burning kisses to fulfill his every fantasy. Malik's tongue stiffened as it penetrated her hole, taking on a lizard-like characteristic, and as if she were a melting chocolate ice cream cone, he took huge swiping licks, purposely grazing her asshole and sending her over the edge like never before.

There was nothing about her that wasn't sexy. Malik had to wish he was part octopus in order to have enough hands to feel her vibe.

Her very own responses suggested that she wanted more friction than a graze, as she reached back pulling her ass cheeks apart while rising up slightly,. He obliged her and began eating her ass out as if she was a delicacy. He tossed her salad better than any Olive Garden.

Mia was gasping for air, finally laying him down on his back. She dug her one-inch fingernails into his muscular chest, drawing a few drops of blood to mark her territory. That was pain immediately followed by the pleasure he felt as she mounted him with no hands needed. He stood erect, allowing her juices to trickle down his pole, and allowing more and more meat to enter her.

She began to cry real tears as he began poking her insides, striking virgin territory. Not giving in to pain, Mia worked her hips slowly, and was determined to take his entire length.

"Oh, my stomach!" she cried out.

Her tightness, beauty, and hot oils tore at the very core of his soul. With every ounce of strength, he tried to hold back. In just a matter of seconds, Malik would scramble her eggs and bring them forth.

Taking back control, he placed both pillows beneath her midsection. Face down, and with her ass in the air, he slid her to the edge of the bed. Malik stood, leaning over her in a push-up position. Stiff as can be, he plunged into her fold, stirrin' it up like coffee.

He begged, "Oh, Mia, back that ass up!" only to be conquered by his body lunging forward. She relinquished, no longer even to hold onto the sheets.

"Malik, don't stop!" she screamed. "Give it to me now! Give me your star! Cum inside of me!"

With that, he began to sprinkle her insides by releasing his entire being. The ceiling fan alone couldn't cool down this type of heat.

Just a few more pumps, plus a kiss, and this would have to be considered "making love". They both collapsed in each other's arms.

Malik said, "By the way, you know I love you, right?"

With a devilish grin, she whispered, "I know you do, especially after all of this!" Then she caressed her firm ass and said "I love you, too!"

******

Then it suddenly dawned on Mia that the house was really quiet and everyone must have left.

She asked, "Malik, did you see my parents when you came in here? We damn sure were making a lot of noise, and my moms don't even play no doors closed in her house."

"Shit, they probably bounced to go get it in themselves. I was locked with your father, and it's been like two decades damn near for him. I know Supreme been overdue!" Malik told her.

"Wow! Picture my moms fuckin'!" Mia thought aloud. She then asked, "Daddy, tell me, how did you get out anyway? I know Born Freedom had to be with you."

Malik confirmed, "He sure was, until we got here. Brian had faked like he took us into custody, and our first stop was Burger King. Then he dropped himself off to get rid of those titties. Born and I went to get my car and his surprise."

"What type of surprise, and where is he at now? You know Jazz got issues, and she and my brother are a hot mess," Mia confided.

"I scooped him a BMW MS before I went in and had it garaged on the low. As far as a hot mess, you ain't ever lied. As soon as we came in, your brother had China girl grindin' on his lap. I guess drinks and a lil' smoke make the world go 'round!"

"So where did you park at, just in case my parents come back?" she asked.

"Right in the driveway. But if she asks whose car, say your Benz. I'm about to go to sleep right here, right now!"

"Go, you!" she said with a smile. "You did say on the bus that you had a Benz when I first met you, remember?" she reminded him.

"You thought I was lying to you just to try to impress you, didn't you?"

"It really didn't matter, because I thought your little swagger was cute. Can you at least put on your boxers?" she reasoned.

"I would if I could, but I was in such a rush to see you that I went commando," he admitted.

169

"Too bad you can't fit these," Mia teased, twirling a pair of red thongs on her index finger.

"Yeah, I bet I would look sexy with a red string running up my ass and my hairy nuts dangling on each side!" he joked.

"Too much information! Let's just get some type of rest. The sun is coming up already," Mia yawned.

******

Judging by the looks of things, D.B.'s plan must have come together. There were naked bodies and empty bottles everywhere. The scent of weed insinuated it was a hella session beyond just to soothe someone's cataracts. It was unclear who did who.

Keisha and Denise were still asleep, tangled up with the twins.

Big Wanda was holding D.B. like a little teddy bear.

April and China had Fred in his bed chained up, with traces of candle wax all over his freaky ass.

It had to have been a good show, because Leeza was asleep in the armchair at the foot of the bed, recording the ceiling with the camcorder.

Good thing Herman and Ruby had gone to Atlantic City as planned. They were listening to the ocean, while the moonlight welcomed traces of the sun, casting a shadow on her hourglass figure. They called her "Big Momma" because of the respect level she demanded—nothing more and nothing less.

# Chapter Thirty

## The Morning After

Born Freedom and Jazz did manage to slip away, ending up back at her place. Just as the sun began to rise, he re-entered her again.

Cunningly, she played like she was asleep. However, just like most women, she knew exactly when to lift up so that her panties could slide right off.

He loved the foreplay and power held over her awaiting body. Allowing just the head to make contact caused Jazz great wetness. While dabbing playfully at her slot, he slicked her asshole by spreading the nectars along the passageway, poking a little deeper each time to test her willingness. With all of his poking and dabbing, the slight grinding rotation of her hips made it quite evident that she'd surrender once again.

A soft moan escaped her as he forced himself deep inside. Slowly, he began pumping her with such strong, deliberate, and equally punishing strokes, she was obviously awake now. Jazz banged back hard to meet him, wanting more and more. For the both of them, this sensation was just too good to prolong.

"Here it is!" she let out as Born's body tensed up to endure their explosions. Seconds later, and already for the third time that morning alone, they dozed right back off to sleep.

******

It was a long night for Stan and Snow White. He had finally convinced her that although he was a DEA Agent, it was all about her. He promised irregardless of her role in the prison scandal, she'd be guaranteed to walk and not even be charged or suspected.

Racing against time to exit under the shadows, they picked up any evidence that would be obvious. Then he began flooding the house with natural gas from the stove.

Now this was a prime example of why you can't believe everything you see on TV.

In the zone, Stan actually acted on a *"What would Steven Seagal do next?"* type of notion. He recalled seeing a movie that showed how Seagal used the microwave oven as a timer. He set it for thirty minutes, put inside a dozen raw eggs still in their shells, along with a half-opened bottle of liquor. Supposedly, the impact from the eggs exploding and the liquor igniting would turn the microwave into a nice fireball mixed with the natural gas, causing a mob-type inferno.

He had already placed the contents of Roger's safe in the rear of his SUV. Their first stop was Snow White's place so they could freshen up and relax a bit while counting their new wealth.

During the time she was in the shower, Stan noticed a girl-on-girl DVD on top of the television. For anyone else, that would've been a plus, but for him and his old fashioned ass, the idea of her going both ways wasn't too thrilling.

However, knowing she was naked in the hot steamy shower had Stan with dick in hand in no time. Debating with himself, he didn't know if he should intrude on her just because the door was open.

Then again, by the time he could make up his mind, he was already looking for something to wipe up his nut before she came out.

******

Word was out and an official count was in. Akbar Shabazz was the only prisoner not accounted for; that is, according to Sondra Tisdale, who was immediately appointed by the governor himself.

Not for nothing, this would be the perfect cover-up to begin forming some type of far truth. Remember, Akbar was really the first person murdered on the inside by C.O. Becca, the Mexican-looking bitch that Brianna ended up smokin' along with Lt. Larry.

However, this type of conspiracy could easily shape rumors into facts. The warden, missing in action, was believed to have aided in the prisoner's escape. The speculation of a sexual relationship would be the motive, being that lately a lot of prominent figures were coming out of the closet.

The community would be relieved to hear of only one escapee on the loose. The bi-sexual orientation somehow took the threat away from it all; those guessing the homophobic mentality relates to passiveness, flowers, and sugar to gay men. Hence, forgetting that "the man" can come out at any given time and they still can cause damage like any other man.

******

Back at San Dora, Smitty, Born C, and Tone anxiously awaited daybreak in the hopes of an early release.

Old School just knew they were out today and packed all of his shit last night. He said, "I'm not leaving shit! So nobody bet' not ask me for shit! Every time I call myself looking out, I end up right back and looking out these goddamn windows. If I'm still here when the sun comes up, they want every day; and I want every tray!"

Speaking of tray, with the kitchen out of order, a cold cereal breakfast was catered in from a nearby county jail.

Sure enough, right after they ate, all four were called out for a legal visit and instructed to bring all of their property. Old School knew the deal. Born C, Tone, and Smitty wondered why they needed all of their property for a legal visit.

"Not so fast!" Smitty yelled his signature saying to the guard. "Why do we need our property for a legal visit? This bet' not be some bullshit!"

The guard responded assumingly, "Shit, after all the ruckus yesterday, y'all going to the motherfuckin' Feds! Watch what I tell ya!"

In single file, they walked, struggling to carry all of their belongings, unsure of what to expect. Some thought betrayal was in the picture. But Old School kept a good vibe, reasoning that it wouldn't be odd for the Feds to want to talk to somebody about all of this. They concluded to plead the fifth and wait out whatever was about to come.

All four sat quietly with patience, waiting to remain silent or begin lying. When the door opened, an almost familiar face appeared. He was wearing a dark blue suit, white button up, accented with a powder gray and blue necktie. It was quite G.Q. for an agent to be standing tall in a pair of gray and blue official Wally Gators. Behind the dark shades would be loads of questions. He cleared his throat, demanding attention, with a five o'clock shadow adding secrecy.

"Good morning, men," rang out in the deep voice. "Or should I say, 'Ha-a-a-ay! How u doin'?'"

Smitty jumped up. "Not so fast!" he shouted, as if he was about to solve the biggest mystery in the world.

Old School blurted out, cutting Smitty off in mid-sentence, "Brianna—I mean Brian! Man, you fooled the shit out of me! You sharp, man! You sharp! Is you pimpin' or the police? Shit! How ya knock dem titties down in one night?" He asked this question dead-ass serious. Throwing a curve, he went on to say, "Real talk, you still got a fat ass for a nigga! Betta stop fuckin' with dem squats or try to walk bowlegged to cut down on that apple bottom! So what's the deal, playboy? We outta here or what? They done fucked me up, talking 'bout we going to the Feds."

"We're good. I'm going to have to cuff and shackle you to

make it look good. For now, we're headed to a DL spot, and not any gay shit either, Old School. Everybody's trying to get together before the night is out to put everything together. We at least got a mil' apiece coming."

Smitty's eyes damn near popped out of their sockets. "You mean mil' like in million, or meal like in eat-eat? 'Cause, shit...I been owed it to myself and it's in my blood to be pimpin' since pimpin' been pimpin'."

Born C said, "A million what? Say word! I'ma get a million dollars!"

Tone wasn't surprised at all, because too much went on for it to be just about some boy pussy.

Brian suggested that they downplay their excitement, and as they were walking out of the facility, he commented with a huge smile, "Shit! I ain't never had a mil' my damn self!"

"Before we get too far, stop by the 'stow' 'cause I need a drank!" Old School made it known.

One year in the bing still didn't take the corners off a square, because Brian unknowingly responded, "There's bottled water in the center console, already cold."

Everyone began laughing, except for Brian, and Old School said, "Damn, junior! I said I needed something to 'drank' not 'drink'! A drank is liquor. A taste is liquor. A shot is a drank or some good pussy. But water is water!"

******

Governor Nulls was the realest you could ever imagine. He lived in the hood and rented out the governor's mansion for functions, and events and funneled the money back to the hood for after school programs. Governor Nulls lived under a fake name with Section 8, and he received food stamps on the EBT card. He stayed strapped and didn't do bodyguards because he was 'bout it. One of his guns was unregistered just in case he had to pop off on the hood shit.

Since it only took five minutes through the shortcut to get to the projects on foot, Governor Nulls grabbed a Dutch, twisted up some 'fruits' (weed), and headed out the door. First stop, the bodega to see Papi and grab a 25¢ bag of salt-n-vinegar potato chips and a 50¢ Guzzler juice for after blazin' one to the face.

Reaching Shekeem's door in no time, banging instead of ringing the doorbell was normal. The Hood News sign out front was written in black magic marker on some silver duct tape, stuck all across the mailbox. This was attached to a paper plate sign reading "Snow Cones, Icee Cups, Blunts, Loosies, and Candy—Rear Window".

Shamik answered the door. "Hi, Uncle Nulls! You already know my lazy brother, 'Keem, is still sleep. I heard him last night trying to creep some chicken up in here. Come on in and do you as usual, and let me touch that Dutch!"

"Naw, boo-boo! You ain't put in on this. Plus, I bet you ain't even wash your face or nothing—out here talking me to death still smellin' like drinks," said her uncle.

Laughing, she replied, "No sir, Uncle. I wasn't even drinking last night. I'm glad you acting all stank with your little 'reg'. I got some 'piff' straight from yard (Jamaica)!"

"Who you get it from? That ugly little—or should I say 'lickle'—yoot that always be smilin'? What dey call 'im; Shabba?" he teased.

"His name ain't Shabba, and I don't know why he's always just-a-smilin'. He ain't' know da gol' toof t'ing been done a'ready," Shamik laughed.

"Yes, my yoot!" he continued to mock with his West Indian accent. "Wake up 'ur bro-da so all a we can make it 'appen, ya 'ear me say? Ay, wompin' wit' 'ur gal, Kizzy?"

Shamik responded with her accent, "Naw sir, man! Un'kill, dat black tack 'head trife'lin'!"

"Me no dis genius. She young an' tenda, too. She tic betta dan da clock. Must be da blood clot music dat get 'er 'ot on t'ing. Rememba late-a an me'll link you wit' a nice propa t'ing late-a."

Shekeem walked into the room, half asleep, hand outstretched and reaching for the piece. "What up, Unc? Let me touch that," he greeted.

"I just told your sister the same thing: Wash your face before you go reaching for shit. Plus, you don't need to be trying to smoke up everything you see, especially since you ain't put in on this," reminded Nulls.

"Alright, Unc, just cool ya'self. Let me turn on everything and get it warmed up. I'll be right back. I just need to throw some water on my face like you said," Shekeem agreed.

"Shit, need to throw some look-good on that face! I don't know where you thought you looked like me at. The eyebrows?" his uncle teased. "Yo, I'm high as hell! Boy, y'all missed some good ass weed..."

# Chapter Thirty-One

## The Game Plan

"Oh shit! Wake up, Ma!" Born said, nudging Jazz.

"What's wrong, Born?"

"Nothing's wrong. I need you to call over to Mia's because I need to wake Malik up. We're supposed to get the Suburban back to Brian so that he could do what he had to do by now."

"Well the phone is right there next to you. Just press *14 and it'll start ringing."

"No doubt."

The phone rang four times before Mia answered with a groggy voice, "Hello."

"Good morning. This is Born Freedom. May I please speak to Malik? We were both supposed to be up by now, but you know…! How was your night?"

"No comment," Mia said mischievously. "Let me wake him up."

"Peace! Peace! This is Malik."

"Peace, God! We need to get it in gear. You know Brian

178

probably needs the 'burban," Born Freedom told him.

"True, true. Yo, meet me at the corner store up the block so we can go to the spot together."

"I feel you." Then he thought to himself, *The spot?* "Don't tell me you done ripped and pulled out the handcuffs to wife her!"

"You already know. Like I ain't get it from you!"

"That you did learn. I'll see you in 'knowledge cipher' (10)."

"True indeed. Peace!"

After hanging up the phone, Malik said, "Listen, Mia. I've got to get the Suburban back to Brian so that he can make some moves. We're about to brainstorm and come up with the ultimate. Get some rest, though, because you all are probably going to have to work today to make it look good."

"As long as the game plan doesn't change from us getting away with everything, I'm good. I'ma go to work and act like I don't know what happened. So will I hear from you before it's time to go?"

"Definitely! As a matter of fact, you'll see me. I need your number, too, so it'll be the first one I save in my new phone," he lied. "Your phone got a camera?"

"Of course! Just be careful." She handed him the paper and said, "Here, I wrote it down for you because after all 'that' I put on you, you might forget your own name!"

"Oh, whateva!" Malik laughed, while kissing her before he left.

******

Checking himself in the rearview mirror, he had to get his game face on. Facing Precious, his son's mother—and still fiancée—could be hell at times. She knew how to work his nerves and push his buttons with little to no effort.

Malik loved Precious and she loved him. For him, the flesh always weakened him, and this is what kept him on her shit list. They'd be apart, but still claiming one another, though. He figured seeing his son, Finess, always made it worth tolerating the 'drama queen'.

Arriving at the corner, Born Freedom was already out of his

truck, pacing. "Yo, what's good, Malik?" he greeted. "You came from the other way, but I drove past the spot and didn't see no truck in the driveway."

"Say word? Stop playin'. You gotta be kiddin' me! I know she didn't get a government truck towed because it was in the driveway."

"You know with the drama queen anything is possible. You did leave a note, didn't you?"

"But I didn't mention the $50,000 truck in the yard with government plates on it. She probably thought the Feds jumped out on us and we're in some more shit. Let's just bounce."

******

Escalade and D.B. had just woken up, both looking hung over and in need of a cold shower.

The twins, One and Two, were still out for the count.

Leeza killed the battery in the camcorder by passing out with it on last night. That DVD had captured some great moments. Hopefully, she brought the cord with her for a little rewind once she got up.

Wanda had been awake discussing with April and China their next move. Denise and Keisha had already left because it was already settled that they'd be working the second shift just in case Jazz and Mia needed backup.

"China, what's up with you and Fred?" asked Wanda. "You know he's fuckin' with Jazz, too, right?"

"It's nothing. As long as I get mines!" China answered sarcastically.

"Well, we don't get down like that unless it's clearly understood mutually. I know she do her thing, too, but when you was all up in his lap last night, I could tell she was feeling some type of way. If looks could kill, we would've had your funeral," Wanda told her.

"I doubt that. That bitch can't see me," China said, trying to convince her damn self.

"Now, China, you know Jazz will get all up in your little egg foo young ass. You know I'ma tell her, don't ya!" threatened Wanda.

"Naw, naw! It ain't like that. Jazz's my girl. I'll holla at her and see if it's a problem. The shit shouldn't be. Did Fred see her sneaky ass dip with that sexy nigga, Free-at-Last, or whatever the hell his name is?" China said, changing the subject.

"You mean Born Freedom?" she inquired.

"Yeah, chile. Now that's who she better be guarding, because he can have all this wonton pussy! Ain't nothing like a thug with some Timbs on! Come to think of it, ain't you and April both done fucked the police? I see Dougie Boy—Do Boy—hell, you know who—be getting it in," China reflected aloud.

April interrupted, salty, "I'm glad da fuck somebody goddamn recognized. I *was* fuckin' him first!"

"Ah, bitch! You and China's triflin' asses were sucking on Fred's dick and balls together last night!" Wanda rudely defended.

"How my pussy taste, hoe?" Directing the comment to Wanda, April set it off.

The pushing and shoving got D.B. and Fred's attention. Poor China was too light in the ass to get caught between the heavyweights.

"What's going on here?" D.B. questioned, while separating the two contenders. "Please, don't everyone speak at once!"

"Your fault, little dick!" China scored with a too-through look on her face.

"Now wait a fuckin' second with the name calling. I know my shit ain't little, you fake-ass karate-movie-looking bitch!"

Fred jumped in with, "Everybody just take a deep breath. We're in shit still up to our elbows, and have to keep our circle tight. No pushing, shoving, or name-calling is necessary. We're a team, and if sex is the cause of all this, then go fuck yourselves!" Fred laughed hysterically, trying to make light of the situation.

"My bad, girl! You know you my bitch," Wanda apologized to April. "Your pussy does taste good, too. Don't it, China?"

"What do you mean by 'Don't it China'?" April asked.

Wanda insisted, "Just wait until we play that DVD back. Last night, we were all drunk as hell. Me and China freaked you last night, and you laid right there enjoying every minute of it, huh, Fred?"

"My name is 'Ben-it' and I ain't in it no more. Can we get an encore to refresh my memory, though?"

"Now that we're all back to being civilized, why don't we wake up everyone and begin going over a few things?" D.B. said, trying to maintain some sort of order.

D.B. continued. "Well, Denise and Keisha are working second shift with Mia and Jazz. That's why they left early. The Twins, Detective St. John, and I have to begin crossing all our t's, and you all can begin dotting the i's. I expect everyone to work their shifts as usual; just keep your eyes and ears open. No drug sales or fucking at work until further notice, please! With this government, somebody is always watching somebody."

Fred reminded, "Yo, Brian said we had some ends coming our way, like in the neighborhood of six or seven figures. When we gonna touch that?"

"I'll discuss that with him this afternoon and get back to you all this evening. We need new cell phones, and there is no time like the present to get them. A lot is going to have to change for a while because with the Feds, it's always an ongoing investigation until it's wrapped up completely."

******

Snow White was still a major issue because her whereabouts were still unknown to everyone. The connection between her and Stan was still their little secret. Some felt that her death would be their only guarantee she wouldn't talk.

******

Using the remote on the sun visor, Malik opened the garage and pulled right in. Born Freedom's loud music more than likely was a dead giveaway to their arrival.

By the time they looked towards the side kitchen door, Precious was already standing there, arms folded and ready for drama.

"Oh, hell no! You two still up to no good! Looks like y'all had some rest last night. In what bitch's bed or hotel room, I don't know! How dumb can you be? You still pop up the next day right around checkout time. And you wonder why both you motherfuckas are on my shit list."

"Good morning to you, too, Precious!" Malik interrupted.

"Fuck a good morning! Did you really think I was finished, stupid? Don't you know where my mother lives?" How come you left a cheesy-ass note instead of bringin' your ass over there last night? Your family's not important to you still, I see. Whoever's truck that was that's gone, too. I don't even know how or who or shit! When I got here, it was here, and a half-hour later it was gone."

Turning to Born Freedom, she asked, "Mr. Freedom, why in da hell did you have your convicted, felony-ass shoes on my motherfuckin' carpet? Then go in my kitchen, knowing you ain't wash hand-the-first? Y'all both remind me of AJ and Free, old asses acting like fuckin' kids. What y'all here for, to watch cartoons?"

Born Freedom didn't say a word. He looked for Malik to handle Precious.

After a minute, the only words of endearment Malik could find were, "I love you, too! Where's Finess?"

"Sleep. Why? You went and made him some brothers and sisters to play with?"

"Not hardly. You know how fan members be blaming babies on us, trying to come-up because we got a couple of dollars, huh, Born?"

"Man, don't get her started back on me! Real talk, we need to find out about the 'burban because the clock is ticking. Let's bounce. I'll drive since I'm already in the driveway."

"What the fuck! You ain't even come in the house and you're leaving already? Oh, I get it. Since your son is sleep, fuck me, right? Wait 'til later when you want some of this fire," Precious said, grabbing her pussy with two hands.

"I'll be right back. I really got to handle something before noon. I'ma explain when I come back," Malik told her from the passenger side window, as they backed out of the driveway rather fast.

Precious thought to herself, with her pussy throbbing, *I'm fuckin' him tonight, though—hard!*

# Chapter Thirty-two

### Go With The Flow

Born Freedom pulled up in front of 72 Mill Street, relieved to see the Suburban parked out front. When Malik and he knocked on the door, it took a while for Brian to answer. The smell of charcoal was in the air, but in the hood, any time was a good time for a barbecue.

After Brian led the two out to the backyard area, they were surprised to see Born C, Tone, and Smitty with Old School gettin' tipsy at the pit. They all embraced, exchanged smiles, and laughs, while reaching for snacks at the same time to nibble on. It ain't a barbecue without the cheapest, biggest bag of plain chips in the store and some hot dogs until the meat gets done.

"I need everyone's attention for a second," Brian said. "I have to go meet Governor Nulls and Special Agent Greene before the news conference. The twins and some of the ladies are on their way over to join y'all. There's plenty of food and beverages, and I expect some ribs by the time we get back. Put your guns up, and if you're gonna smoke, look upstairs. We confiscated some good-ass weed. Just smoke it outside. The neighbors ain't gonna say shit. They're hiding from the mob, Escobar, and the real Noriega!

******

It was 11:45 a.m. by the time Brian had reached the Hood News studio. Special Agent Greene had only been there a couple of minutes. He seemed upset that the governor was high as hell and about to appear on national TV.

"Chill out, D.B.! This ain't the first time I've been on TV fucked up. How do you think I think straight? You see, New Jerusalem and Cali are the only states where we burn it down. Even the doctors are with the bullshit. You ain't never seen so many niggas with cataracts, feel me? You gotta loosen up. I realize you back on official business and shit, but fuck dat 'round here, playboy! I got your back, feel me?"

Brian insisted on organizing a plan, but the clock said "no". Without warning, Shekeem began counting, while the cameras panned in and Shamik said:

"Good afternoon, and welcome once again to Channel 77 News. You may have heard through the grapevine the gossip and speculation that Akbar Shabazz is the only inmate not accounted for. Rumor has it that Warden Brown aided in the prisoner's escape and their secret was out. Yes, it appears to have been a sexual relationship between the two, and there's more that went on behind the iron door.

"Governor Nulls, could you inform us on the status of your investigation and the details on how things unfolded? Also, how and why you decided to appoint Sondra Tisdale as the new acting warden. Oh, and I see you have two distinguished law enforcement officers with you this afternoon, as well."

"Well, first of all, Shamik, and to all the viewers at home, As Salaam Alaikum, which means peace be with you.

"Now to elaborate on your first pile of questions, the investigation is going well in its first twenty-four hours. These fine officers with me, Special Agent Douglas Greene and Detective Brian St. John, have been remarkable.

"We already were building a case against the warden based on previous information and complaints we received of inappropriate sexual contact he was forcing upon male officers and inmates at San Dora. We dug deep and found that over two decades ago there were allegations that Mr. Brown had even molested his own son. However, he was never convicted, and that investigation ended inconclusively.

"Now, regarding Mr. Shabazz and his escape, we only can conclude that at least two of three things must have happened: One is, Mr. Shabazz could have already been out of the facility and hadn't had the chance to sneak back in before all the chaos. Or two, Warden Brown was overpowered by Shabazz and there might just be a hostage situation.

"My third scenario is the two were lovers and butt buddies staged everything and ran off into the sunset. Shit, who the hell knows? What is for sure is that I know is that nigga owes me twenty dollars!"

"Governor, please don't start already! We're on national TV, live!"

"Okay, Shamik. Y'all talk to her and tell her what's good!" the governor said, turning it over to Special Agent Greene and Agent St. John.

"Good afternoon, everyone. I am Special Agent Douglas Green with the United States DEA. We've been conducting an intense investigation regarding heavy drug trafficking over the years at San Dora. Warden Brown is believed to have benefited by the millions.

"Yes, we're actually not talking a few balloons

swallowed at a visit, or those with outside clearance and furloughs cuffin' (smuggling it up their ass) things. We're talking organized crime family members working in cahoots with the warden and guards to maintain a lucrative operation inside and out. Detective?"

"Good afternoon. I'm Detective Brian St. John, and I've been the closest to this investigation. I say that because I've been inside, undercover and left for dead for a little over a year. What started as a sex scandal allowed me to stumble across the billion-dollar drug trade going on. I sound bitter because I am, and I'd like to thank Governor Nulls for personally risking his own life to come inside and rescue me. Not that I was in any danger from the prisoners, because I was a convict myself.

"I've learned that a Black man with a badge is still considered a nigga and expendable, because I never signed up to go under for over a year. I was left there…

"The sad part of it all, the entire file was destroyed in the fire and I'll just have to report on the sexual incidents that I'm certain of instead of speculate the intricate details of the latter.

"I'd like to also make an announcement while I have everyone's undivided attention. As soon as I submit my official report, I'll be turning in my shield because I have had a change of heart. Instead of increasing the prison population with my own people, I'd rather take on preventative measures to free us. My name's being changed to Equality Born Unique. That will be all. Thank you."

"Wow! Now for all the viewers at home, I have one question: Do you like fruit? Well, how did you like those apples?" Shamik laughed. "You've heard it here first. Equality Born Unique may have lost his entire investigation on a disc due to the fire, but he found his righteous self by being amongst the Gods. Now that's news!"

"Governor Nulls, isn't that the best news we've heard all day? And you still never said why you appointed Sondra Tisdale as acting warden."

"That was real good news that the brother found his true self by "A"-alike. Now do you really want the truth about Ms. Tisdale and her appointment?"

"Hello! This is live news. Of course we want the truth," Shamik reminded.

"No beepin' then if I tell you, okay?"

"Okay!"

"Sondra fine as hell and thicker than a motherfucka.. Shit! I'll wife that!"

"Let me find out the governor thinks this is the *Love Connection*. I do enjoy the hot gossip, although this ain't the beauty shop. Shekeem, what do you think about all this?" asked Shamik.

"First of all, I'd like to thank you and our guests for allowing upfront and exclusive news. Now to express my personal views.

"Equality Born Unique, that was a power move to accept your Black self. That's the best news to me. Peace to all the Gods and Earths worldwide.

"It seems like the investigation is going to be missing a lot of pieces to the puzzle because of that disc that got destroyed in the fire. Plus, with the warden missing, hiding, or somewhere naked, ain't no telling what the real truth is.

"The sad part is, if either or both Akbar Shabazz or Warden Brown has been murdered, it'll end up another unsolved case. Since when do they *really* investigate Black on Black crime?

"Governor Nulls, let me find out Sondra got you open. I thought you was a playa!" Shekeem said.

"I was a gentleman before a playa, and you always

make your next move your best move. In life, the only good shortcut is taking corners off a square, 'cause if it's meant to be, what goes around comes around—if it's a real circle!" Governor Nulls replied.

"I should've known you had a good answer. Thank you and thank everyone for watching. This has been Shekeem reporting for Channel 77 News."

"Yo, is that camera off? Dem lights hotter than I don't know what! I bet they burn a lot of electric. What your bill be looking like?" asked the governor.

"Yours, because our shit included with the rent," Shekeem said, laughing hysterically.

"I know that's right! What y'all about to get into?" Governor Nulls asked.

Equality said, "There's a barbecue on Mill Street. You know Born C, Smitty, Tone, and Old School are out already. I grabbed them first thing this morning to *interrogate* (wink-wink)."

"That's nice. What can I bring to the cookout?" asked D.B.

The whole room got quiet and he couldn't understand why.

"Hood rules are there's a difference between "cookouts" and "barbecues". At a cookout, you all chip in and bring a little of this and that, and a little meat for the grill. A couple of people help out grillin'. When the food is finished grillin', you all make plates and eat as if it's one big meal. That ain't no barbecue," Equality explained.

"At a barbecue, you bring your hungry ass and plan on eating all damn day. Ain't no grill in sight. There's a homemade barbecue pit with ribs, chicken, hot dogs, sausages, burgers, and steaks. There's a pot of homemade sauce and a fork with a torn piece of white cloth wrapped around it that you dip in the sauce to "mop" your meat with. The way you mop your meat is to slap sauce on it while it's cookin'. Unlike on a grill, where you pour some bullshit out of a bottle on your meat once it's on your plate.

"There's only one chef, and it's usually the oldest man with the most experience and stories to tell while he's "Q-ing".

"At a barbecue, there's macaroni salad and potato salad. At a cookout, there's tossed salad. You see, niggas don't eat brown lettuce, and leaving tossed salad out on a table all day…you already know! So I guess eventually D.B. will see the difference when he gets there."

Finally, Equality said in response to D.B.'s question, "Just bring some new bitches!"

Shamik said, "Excuse you! There's a lady in the room!"

"No disrespect, sista. You know how we—"

"No, I don't know how we do. Brothas be killin' me with that. You don't find it a problem calling women bitches, but you come from a woman. Without knowledge of self, the devil's ways have turned the God inside out, and this is why a man is considered a dog. However, since you don't lift your leg to piss or your finger to uplift our present condition, you must squat and piss, making *you* the bitch!"

"Wow! That's peace," concluded Governor Nulls. "Let's just build from that error, shall we, by getting up in a few at the barbecue, get our eat on, and all that. Word?"

"That sounds like a plan," Equality Born Unique agreed, happy to get out of Shamik's line of fire. "We need some jacks (phones), too, like yesterday."

"Need to find out if the meat done 'cause I got the munchies," joked the governor.

"I'll try to reach my superior, Stan, before the barbecue, smooth him out and shit. I know he's seen the news just now. He's like family to me. Plus, dead presidents make history repeat itself. We may not be slaves, but enough zeroes caused by dead presidents can still buy a nigga!" D.B. said, the only one laughing at his slave ship mentality.

******

After everyone left, the governor stayed behind and waited for Shamik and Shekeem to get ready for the barbecue. In the hood, nobody turned down good, free food. Plus, he could tell

191

from earlier, based on their facial expressions, there was going to be some off-the-record questions.

"Who got my red lighter?" Shamik asked. "I had it right here on the bathroom sink. Uncle Nulls, you were the only one who came and used the bathroom. Plus, you left the toilet seat up."

"Alright, 'Sherlock Homegirl', you got me. But why all the crazy looks earlier?"

"'Cause you with the bullcrap! All y'all with the same bullcrap! I know a lie when I hear one. So what's the deal? This ain't got nothing to do with no breaking news or governor this and that. I'm talking straight fam on this. Just let us know; how can we be down? Right, Shekeem?"

"You already know I need a good come-up. I'm down for whatever and the media persuades the masses—hello! Just let us know how y'all want the story told. Feel me, Unc?"

"I feel ya. Right now, shit going on in a big way. Yo, I'm talking pure bullshit. People are dead, missing, or lying like a rug. If it wasn't for so damn much money, I wouldn't even be with this B.S. But Equality is my main man from back in the day. On the low, he hood. Now when he say 'mils' involved, he ain't talking about eat-eat. That nig—I mean brotha—is smart as hell with that computer love. I bet he done wired money into all types of untraceable offshore accounts. Ain't no disc burnt up in no fire, but that was some quick thinking. So, y'all in?"

"That's like asking is water wet. You already know. Cha-ching! Bling-bling! Feel me?" Shakeem replied.

"That's what's up, Unc!" Shamik then asked, "Can I drive your Benz?"

"I got one better. Since we're about to blow, you can have it—but here's the deal. When we get right, you have to buy me and your brother any rims we like."

Almost tackling him, Shamik dove on her uncle, giving him a big hug and anxiously agreeing to an offer she couldn't refuse. Then Nulls and Shekeem rushed out the door.

# Chapter Thirty-Three

## Back to Work

"Good afternoon, everyone. As you may have guessed or heard by now, I'm Sondra Tisdale, the New H.N.I.C., oka-a-a-y! Let's get a few things straight right now!

"I don't sweat small shit, and snitches get stitches. Whatever was going on before me stops right the fuck now!

"I don't give a fuck about no union, no grievances, or none of that other bullshit. I'll fire your ass without pay and jam your ass up so hard you'll be appealing shit until the cows come home. So, don't get it twisted.

"I only fucks with those that are 'bout it, because I'm 'bout it-'bout it my damn self."

She turned her back to everyone seated and sarcastically asked, while pointing over her shoulder, "Is the back of my shirt dirty?" Then she answered both of her own questions. "Then I must ain't said nothing wrong then. Do you while I do me, now play wit' it. I'll bus' your shit to the white meat. Dismissed!"

Jazz was turned on by that introduction. Everyone else

cleared out quickly, shook by their new supervisor's introduction. Holding Mia slightly by the arm, along with Keisha and Denise's presence, Jazz approached the newly appointed acting warden, and commenting aloud, she began, "Alrightee then, Ms. H.N.I.C.! Congratulations! My name is—"

"You're Jazz, Mia, Denise, and Keisha," said Sondra. "I can't get no dap!"

They were all surprised to see Sondra was really 'bout it-'bout it, big sister O.G. status.

"So you're the Ms. S from Connecticut that I heard about," Jazz said quizzically.

"Baby girl, I'm from the 'Beat'. That's what we call Hartford."

"But I always thought your last name was something else."

"It was, but I had a couple of warrants from back in the day and a sista had to remix. That's my name now, like that's her hair!"

They all started laughing at another officer who just entered the room and had one of those long ponytail extensions that was straight as hell, but her head was nappy.

Switching the conversation to a more professional context, they began discussing their posts for the evening and assisting with the (mock) investigation. This allowed all four to work the block together.

******

Denise and Keisha worked the bubble while Mia and Jazz grabbed garbage bags and went to clean out Born Freedom's cell of his personal effects that were left behind.

Jazz bee-lined to the desk, sorting through all of his female pictures he had accumulated over the years. Being the diva that she was, she considered every one of those pictures ugly compared to her.

There was nothing spectacular to Mia going on inside of a cell. She felt betrayed and kind of disappointed that Malik never contacted her at all before work, let alone stopped back by. Yet, she convinced herself there had to be or better be a good explanation.

Moving along after what took about an hour to clear out, snooping in Brianna's old cell was next. Now this cell looked and smelled feminine. The bed was neatly made and the pillows were fluffy and pastel colored. The desk looked like makeup central, but there were no pictures or mail, though.

While stripping the bed, Mia came across a note that was hidden, stuck to the mattress. Curiosity and the heart designs caught her interest. Unbeknownst to Jazz, Mia read the note dated almost a year ago. It read:

Dear Brianna:

I usually don't be getting down like this. But, damn, ma! Between all this time and fine as you are, I've been feeling some type of way. On the down low, what's really good with me and you? I got a few connects and can make your time real sweet here.

So holla at your boy and let me put you under my wing. I really be dreaming about that fat ass and lovely breasts. I wish we had double cells. I'd make sure we were cellies.

It's hard for you right now.

Feeling some type of way,
Born Freedom

Mia stood shocked and quickly slipped the note into her pocket. She wasn't sure whether she should tell Jasmine or what. All types of shit were running through her mind. *Born Freedom on the down low! Wow! I wonder does Malik know. Are they butt buddies? How do I ask? Who do I tell? I wonder does he prefer anal sex—even with Jazz.*

"Girl, you in a daze," Jazz startled her. "Mia, back to earth!"

"I'm with you. I was just thinking about how all these men be locked up without pussy. Do they turn gay or keep secrets amongst themselves?"

"Who knows? I know I ain't fuckin' with no one on the downlow shit unless it's R Kelly himself. I don't know, though, since you mentioned it. Born Freedom can fuck, and I know I got some good pussy, but he do be fucking me in the ass more than anything. I'm gonna have to give his ass the finger test."

"What's the finger test?"

"If a man sucks his thumb, he'll suck a dick. And if you poke him in the ass with one finger, he's a freak, which is a good thing because his dick gets harder. But two, three, four fingers, or a fist, he sweeter than grape Kool-Aid in the projects!"

******

D.B. tried reaching Stan again and finally he picked up.

"Yeah, Doug!" Stan began.

"I've been trying to reach you all morning. I'm sure you've seen the news by now," Doug said.

"I'm afraid not. All morning I've been at the cell phone store because mine took a swim when I was getting in the car. Out of all the places, right smack dab in a puddle."

"Well, if it wasn't for bad luck, we'd have none," Doug pointed out.

"I totally agree."

"Hey, Stan, as a matter of fact, are you still at the phone store now?" asked Doug.

"In the parking lot. Why?"

"Because we all need new phones, and, ah… since you're already there, could you pick us up about ten prepaid and some minutes, and we'll reimburse you?"

"How about I make it my gift to you all for making the last few days a living hell for me?"

"Come on, Stan. You know I'll make it up to you. And we did say we're sorry. Whatever happened to all's well that ends well?" Doug tried to reason.

"Okay, since you're twisting my arm. Where you guys going to be at?"

"We're at 72 Mill Street, having a barbecue."

"Good, because I haven't eaten squat today. I'll see you within the hour."

"Okay, see you then, Stan."

"Alright, goodbye."

# Chapter Thirty-Four

**Trust No One**

"Look what the cat just dragged in, Finess!" Precious said, pointing at Malik. "You're just in time to tell him goodnight, because you and I need to talk! You've been gone all damn day—wait! Finess, tell Daddy goodnight 'cause he about to hear it from me!"

"Okay, Mommy," he said. "Goodnight, Daddy! See ya later!"

"Oh, I don't get a kiss no more?" Malik asked, bending down with open arms to embrace him.

"Not a long one," Finess playfully said, laughing and trying to kiss Malik as quickly as possible.

"You tell 'em, Finess!" Precious joined in. "We don't know where you mouth been at!"

"Don't tell him that! Goodnight, son. I'll see you in the morning. I love you!"

"Love you, too!" Finess said, heading to his bedroom.

******

The living room was silent. Precious and Malik exchanged stares, neither knowing where to begin.

"So, Mr. Malik, you finally got rid of your butt-buddy," she began. "I've been waiting for at least a courtesy call. Then again, I should've known not to expect shit out of you. Where have you been? You look full, because you damn sure didn't eat here today," she continued, making a sniffing sound with her nose. "You smell like you've been at a cookout. But don't you worry. I got just the thing for you to eat for dessert."

"You got on too many clothes to be talking to me," teased Malik. "I don't wanna talk!"

As opportunity knocked, she answered by grabbing him by the hand and leading him to their favorite meeting place... the bedroom.

Seductively, Precious insisted, "Make yourself comfortable. I have a special treat that you almost didn't get."

Stepping out of her sweatpants and T-shirt revealed some of the sexiest lingerie one could imagine. Slipping her feet into her clear heels and directing his feverish gaze to the stage she had installed today just for him, the music began to play.

As if on cue, Precious began climbing the brass pole. Reaching the top, she spread her legs and turned upside down. T-Pain's lyrics directed a perfect show. As the words said, so did she do: "Got the body of a goddess! Got those eyes butter pecan brown. I see you, girl, coming down from the ceiling to the floor!"

Landing in a split, with her hands unleashing his manhood, she whispered, "Let's do the right thing!"

Climbing on the bed, while Malik stood to completely undress, Precious spread wide, inviting him to dessert.

Starting at her feet, he nibbled his way upward to the center of her gravity. She guaranteed to make it go up and down like never before. Yet, before entering, he had to eat his way into her good graces. In no time, his face was soaked with her juices. Having given herself to no other man ever, she had to be fulfilled.

Caressing his smooth, muscular back and running her fingers freely through his hair, she closed her eyes in anticipation of his forceful entry.

Before long, they were panting, totally spent. Precious was content lying there with her head upon his chest, nestling in search of the perfect spot to fall asleep. That is, until she felt some sort of scar tissue on his chest. Without warning, she jumped up out of the bed and turned on the brightest light in the room to further her investigation.

By the time Malik knew what was going on, he had definitely failed inspection.

"You got some fuckin' nerve! How could you already be fuckin' up when you haven't even been out twenty-four hours yet? Are you retarded or just that stupid!" she screamed.

"What are you talking about?" Malik asked, while reaching for the covers.

"You don't know? Playa-playa!"

"Know what?" he wondered, still not having a clue.

"Know that I ain't got no damn nails. So how in the fuck did you get scratches on your chest? Look at that shit! Look like a bitch just dug her mails in you like you're single!" Precious was fuming.

Looking in the mirror, then at Precious, then back to his chest, and then to her hands, Malik was at a loss for words.

Precious stormed out of the bedroom, crying. Once again, she turned on the shower with every intention of washing away Malik's betrayal. By the time she finished accepting her own dumbness and went to confront her pain, Malik was gone without a trace, apology, or goodbye.

Looking in the mirror and talking to herself, crying once again, she said, "Trust no one!"

******

"Hi, Stan."

"Hello, Snow!"

"I've been waiting on your call," she said.

"I would've called earlier from the cookout, but too many ears were around," he said.

"I understand."

"But I did get you something today."

"What is that, Stan-the-Man?" she teased.

"I picked you up a new cell phone since I was in the store, and grabbed a few for everyone else."

"Will I see you tonight, Stan? Because I could use a little lovin'," Snow asked.

"If you look out your window, you could see me now."

"Why you!" she laughed. "Come on in!"

Once inside, Stan presented her with the new cell phone and updated her on what went on that day. She was definitely a hot topic, but he held back on most of the truth. He basically was preserving the mood, and telling her how everyone wanted her dead wasn't the brightest idea.

After a good romp in the sack, he'd eventually try to mention them going out of state during their pillow talk.

"Hey!" Stan began. "You know we got a nice piece of change out of Roger's place. That and including what we could pool together, we'd be all set. I was thinking someplace tropical. How about Hawaii?"

"After all I've been through, I was thinking another country. With your connections, can't you get me a new identity that would remain confidential?" Snow asked, concerned.

"Of course, I can. By the way, what is your name? I feel kind of weird calling you Snow White. It's kind of animated, like 'Baby'."

"My first name ain't Baby. It's Janet. 'Ms. Jackson, if you're nasty!'" she sang like the song.

"Seriously, what is your government name? You know, the one on your paycheck."

"Here's my purse. Look on my driver's license."

"I'll be damn! Your name *is* Janet Jackson!"

"Stan, your cell phone is vibrating," Snow pointed towards the nightstand.

After seeing the Caller I.D., he signaled for her to excuse him while he took the call in private. He whispered to her as if before answering the phone he could be heard, "It's the office!" while tipping into the next room to answer.

"This is Stan. What's going on, Chief?"

"Hello, Stan-the-Man! I see you're up to no good."

"And I see you're eavesdropping, too!" Stan snapped.

"You leave me no choice. One of us has to do our job," said the Chief.

"Well, since you're on your job, sir, Chief, is there any other way to resolve this matter? Because Douglas and the twins are really good men; just caught up in a bad situation."

"Look! They needed ten phones, and we gave them ten phones. It's just that we'll be recording every last word, whether the phone is on or off, with minutes or not, we'll have the last say. You have a choice: Save yourself and Janet Jackson—your Snow White—or go down with the ship. It's your life, sink or swim."

While still engaged in the phone conversation, Snow White came into the room concerned about the lengthy phone call and asked, "Are you okay in here, Stan?"

With sweat pouring from everywhere, he nodded to acknowledge her question and put up one finger to mean he would be right with her.

"Okay, Chief, I'll be in about ten to work out the pension for my retirement and the identification change for Ms. Jackson."

"Make it nine before I change my mind and lock all of your asses up and throw away the key!" the Chief stated, and then hung up.

"Honey, what was that all about?" Snow asked Stan.

"It was good news for us all," he lied. "Everything is going just as planned. We'll be out of here by the end of the week," Stan said, trying to sound reassuring.

"Stan, I heard something out back! Didn't you?" she asked in a panic. "Wait! The neighbor's dog never barks for nothing!" she whispered, holding on to his arm for comfort.

Just then, the window shattered loudly in the living room. Stan dove to cover Snow, hit the switch, turning the light off, and drawing his sidearm.

Snow reached under the bed and pulled out an assault rifle with a banana clip holding fifty rounds of .308 hollow points…

******

Outside of Snow White's apartment, Jazz and Mia lay in the cut, waiting for Wanda's signal to enter. For the last two days, her place had been under surveillance, and they knew she'd be dumb enough to be at home.

After figuring out that Roger was the inside federal agent affiliated with Warden Brown, finding his dead body and the paper trail unscathed made it that much easier to put it together.

Having her father back in her life was still hard to believe, but what he warned her about was unbelievable!

Stan Green was a man not to be trusted. He not only left her father, Herman, holding the bag, but he slept with his own brother's wife, and Douglas isn't supposedly his nephew. Blood tests back then were not as accurate as DNA tests are today.

We shall see, though, because when it comes to sex, "wrap it up", 'cause you can't trust NO ONE!

# Chapter One

I read somewhere people are born into this world with the burden of a sinful nature. That's why when we're young and our siblings get more attention, we tend to go through feelings and feel an awkward way. The question is, what is it that you feel? Is it a sin? What did you do when you had those feelings? Did you cry and throw a temper tantrum, tell yourself how much you hate your family and curse the day you were born, only to get your ass spanked, yelled at, and sent to your room?

"Get your bad ass in there and don't come out until you know how to act!"

I do know how to act; I've always known how to act. I just always wanted a little more attention.

My mother named me Sincere. I hated that name because it always felt like some kind of curse and the first three letters never helped when I thought about it. My mother told me it was a strong name and I should honor it by being an honest, hard worker. Hard Worker psssp! Honest pssp! She wanted me to be just like my father, the hardest working man who left her ass before I was born. In his absence, she wanted me to live up to everything that he didn't. FUCK THAT…the only blue print I needed to follow was mine. More was my mission and more was what I planned to get.

******

I grew up in Yonkers, New York, a place quite different with a different kind of experience that you wouldn't actually get if you lived in the five boroughs. Being in Yonkers, you got the fringe benefits of the fast city life, the new trends, clubs, food, sporting events, and the restless city nightlife. You had all that at the tip of your fingers and then you had Yonkers, a little grimier and politically charged by racist, red neck cops and judges that don't need trees to hang a motherfucker. Yonkers definitely breeds the hardest streets. When you're living and suffering at the same time you gotta go hard. That's where my story starts, in a part of Yonkers that has a unique entity within its self.

My hood, Slow Bomb Projects A.K.A. the Hole, was one of the toughest projects that I knew of. It has a creek that runs through it, the kind of creek that got trash dumped into it every day and I didn't mean kitchen trash. I could remember times as a youngster playing with my little homies, seeing all the traumatizing shit and coming across everything that a kid shouldn't see in that creek. As I came of age, I learned that you ain't seen nothing, you don't know nothing, and you bet not say nothing or somebody might come across you in that creek.

I have a small family compared to the average family in the hood. It was my mother, older brother, myself, and for a moment she went through the phase of having any nigga that wanted to play the role of her man. Most of the guys she wasn't feeling, she just brought them around to provoke my brother. He always bumped heads with the men she was seeing. If my mother were a car, my brother would be the security system Viper. To make matters worse, Pharaoh was a well-respected and highly feared drug lord on the streets. Pharaoh never took shit from anybody, especially when it came to his money. Once I entered a building in the projects where we lived and witnessed Pharaoh and his goons administering a vicious beat down. You get guys that are so

2

fucking stupid that they signal their own death. The guy actually thought that he could get away with tampering Pharaoh's bags of dope. It didn't take long for Pharaoh to find out.

They never even noticed my small frame ease into the building. I stood there in shock as hell watching my brother and his goons beat the life out of old boy. I knew my brother wasn't a good guy, but I didn't know that he was that bad. "Moose, how the fuck did he get in this building? You're supposed to be watching the door!" Pharaoh shouted. "Sincere, take your little ass up stairs….NOW!"

I had to snap out of my trance before Pharaoh's sharp words registered. As I walked pass the slightly conscious man he grabbed my leg, begging for help I couldn't give 'em. I struggled to break his tight grip. "Get off me!" I cried out.

His grip withered when Pharaoh brutally shoved the barrel of the gun into his mouth, shattering his teeth. They made the same sound hitting the floor like when I use to drop my lemonheads. They continued their vicious assault as I shrugged my way down the hallway towards the elevator with my hands trembling in fear. I was shook. I couldn't even push the button. Those type of memories stick with you forever.

******

We were well known throughout the hood because of Pharaoh. He had the drug game on lock and was one of the most paid niggas in the hood. Everybody knew Pharoah, he was well respected on the streets and known for wearing a lot of gold like Pharaohs wore in the Egyptian days. He always reminded me of Mr. T because of all the jewelry he wore around his neck. But he didn't look like Mr. T. Pharaoh had style he was always fresh to death, fly Fila sweat suit, matching Kango tilted over some gazelle frames. I think his smooth chocolate skin, chinky eyes, and deep voice win over the ladies. They use to call the house all night bugging my mother.

"You bitches need to stop calling my house, I keep telling ya'll Terrell doesn't live here, get a life!" That would come after

3

about the tenth call. Then the verbal assassination would get worse. My mother said she named my brother after my uncle. He died before I was born.

Growing up in the hood was like having a full time job and being a full time student. Once you became of age, you had to stay on the grind to survive and learn from your everyday experiences all at the same time. For the kids that were exposed to the game at an early age, the game was all you knew and all you tried to learn was more about the game. Being that we all ran the same crowd and learned the same rules we all knew who was who and who couldn't be trusted. Everybody had a brother or a family member that was married to the game and being that my brother ran things in the hood. I had the ups over every other little nigga trying to come up and I felt that one day all the shit would be mine.

Most of my little homies big brothers worked for Pharaoh and were all a part of the click. After school we would gather where they would be hustling and watch everything. I guess you could say we were taking lessons. It was mandatory that we picked up everything because we used it on the kids that we went to school with, they were the lames and we were the in kids. We watched how they walked, how they talked, how they wore there clothes, how they conducted business and most of all how they made moves on females. We learned the game and we learned it well, nothing went unnoticed. If we were lucky we might get to make a store run for one of them and get hit off a few dollars for going. If business was good and the police wasn't sweating them too much, they might even kick it a bit and hit us off with food and money. Normally it was whatever Chinese food they didn't eat, but we didn't care, we felt part of the crew.

When we had their attention it was the perfect time to show that we were the coolest little niggas in the projects. We showed off everything we knew. We wrestled, slapped boxed, and if any of us had any special kind of talent we made it a point to show it off. For instance Ta Da Head could backwards flip off damn near anything, Merk was good at drawing so his graffiti was everywhere in the projects, Tipsy was a clumsy motherfucker who could never get shit right, and me, I could rap and they loved to

4

hear me spit some shit plus, I was Pharaoh's little brother so that got me even more respect.

Sometimes they would send Tipsy to the store just to see how bad he would fuck up. If he lost money, forgot shit, or just didn't come back at all. Since his mother was a crack head and he stayed out all times of the night everybody just assumed he was doing some type of drugs too. That's why they gave him the nickname, Lil' Tipsy.

Pharaoh warned his crew about letting me hang around when they were hustling, so they were always nervous because they knew if Pharaoh caught me out there with them, some shit was definitely about to pop off. They would always toss me money and tell me to break bread with my little homies and keep it moving somewhere else. But we still hung around anyway. Splitting the money with my crew gave me a little taste of what power felt like. It felt good to know that Pharaoh's soldiers knew what my name was and recognized me as one of them. I remember the night my brother first gave me my street name, it's something that I would never forget.

It was a Friday night and my crew was over my house to stay the night. My moms went out to play cards like she always did on Fridays. So we were chill'n in the house, bugging out like and playing video games. Then, Pharaoh comes storming in the house yelling out orders and shit, telling my friends to get the fuck out. I thought it would die out because he normally got hyper when he caught me goofing off or playing video games, he told me if I wanted to play games to go to the park and play. My friends knew his flip mode so we had a routine, they'd leave and chill on another floor and when he was gone they'd come back up. This time was different, he told me to go and get dressed.

Something was different about him. He was speeding, his eyes were wide open, and his face looked flushed, but I still managed to get dressed in a hurry and put my sneakers on real quick. I couldn't miss the opportunity to ride in my brother's all black Jeep Cherokee  with custom-made interior with the Kenwood base box that a make your heart skip a beat. Pharaoh was out in front of the building waiting on me. As we pulled off I watched my little homies through the side view mirror and I couldn't help but feel sorry for leaving them behind. Oh well, there would be other times to chill with my homies, because this time I was chill'n with my brother. My sympathy quickly began to fade as we bopped our heads in tune to Slick Rick "Hey Young World."

"Now, listen you lil' motherfucker" Pharaoh said as he turned down the music. "How you left your little homies back there was some real foul shit. Had you said fuck it I'm not going, I would have respected that and let you stay with them. Instead, you was thinking of yourself and not your entire crew. Loyalty is everything amongst friends, never leave your men behind no matter what. Is that understood?"

"Yes, Pharaoh," I uttered as he turned the music back up and continued to ride.

As I watched out the window at the movement of the fast nightlife, blood pumped through my veins and my heart began to race at the thought of being a part of it all. On one corner, I saw a bunch of dudes huddled together shooting dice. On the other corner, I saw a bunch of dudes pulled over in a Benz talking shit to some girls. The night air seemed to electrify everything that was going on and to top it all off, I was the center of attention riding through the streets of New York in one of the tightest Jeeps around, or at least I thought I was. But really, maybe it was the loud thumping of the music that grabbed everybody's attention. Looking at the New York City skyline while we were driving on the highway was even a better treat. All the lights and fast cars on the highway gave me a rush and made me feel as if I was about to do something big.

We finally pulled up in front of a house that looked like a castle. It had huge windows that opened up like doors and the entire house was made of fine masonry brick and stucco. The entrance had security doors with a black security gate. I hopped out the jeep wondering where we were and who was on the inside of this castle that I had never seen before.

I looked up and saw Pharaoh on his cell phone and heard him say, "Open the door, Boo."

Shortly after the door opened, a familiar voice greeted us as we walked in. It was Pasha, Pharaoh's girl. She wore a sky blue nightie that was cut very short, revealing a perfect pair of thighs. Her silky jet-black hair complemented her caramel skin, her eyes were pretty and seductive and her smile always made me feel like she belonged to me. Pasha rarely came to my projects but whenever she did she made it a point of making me feel real special. She always made my day by bringing her little sister, Laura.

"Hi, Sincere," Pasha said as we looked and blushed at each other. "Are you hungry? I got some pizza in the kitchen, follow me," she said as she walked in the opposite direction.

Pharaoh mysteriously vanished somewhere in the house while I followed Pasha to the kitchen. The layout to the kitchen was tight; it had a restaurant look with a big table in the middle of the floor surrounded by chairs that looked like thrones suited just for a king. In the center of the table was a basket filled with fresh fruit. I sat at the table while Pasha served me pizza.

"Sincere, you know my little sister is always asking about you."

"For real?" I responded. "Is she here?"

"No, but don't worry you will be seeing her more often now that I am living a little closer to New York."

Pharaoh entered the room with a joint of weed burning between his lips. He passed the joint to Pasha as he pulls her close, locking lips while squeezing her on the ass. She let out a moan that got me excited.

I followed Pharaoh down a short hallway and into another spacious room that had walls painted in strawberry red with big gold trimmed mirrors hanging from them. In the middle of the room was a gold trimmed glass table surrounded by, three plush red butter soft leather chairs. The fireplace was lit and above it was a picture of Pharaoh and Pasha. The carpet was all white and above the huge table hung a crystal chandelier.

I immediately began to take my shoes off in fear of dirtying the carpet, but Pharaoh responded by saying, "Chill out, baby boy. The carpet is stain resistant and besides that, Pasha takes very good care of her Pharaoh's palace. Go ahead park yourself on the sofa I have something that I want to show you."

He left the room for a minute but returned with this huge black suitcase that he laid on top to the cocktail table. I could not help but wonder what was in the suitcase. He opened it and to my surprise, it was filled with more money than I had ever seen in my life.

"You don't get in the game to buy a bunch of clothes and shit and you don't get in the game to attract a bunch of greedy bitches that's there one day and gone the next. You get in the game for one purpose and one purpose only and that's to make a lot of muthafuck'n money. This money will get you and momma out of that slum ass ghetto that we call home, something that our punk ass father couldn't do. Look, little brother, my business is getting bigger and I'm making more money than I ever made before. You see this fly ass house and this plush shit that I got? A few years ago, I would have never imagined that I could achieve all this, but I did and it's all because I don't bullshit and I'm true to my game. It wasn't until I took myself serious that I stepped my game up and that is why I'm calling you Serious from now on. I want you to take everything in life seriously. Whatever it is that you want to do in life, whether good or bad, be serious about it. Now, I know you will respect that name to the fullest. If you don't respect that name then no one else will, you hear me?"

"Yeah I hear you."

He reached in his pocket and pulled out a neatly folded bill. He quickly opened it and buried his nose in it, taking a long, deep snort. With the other hand, he wiped his nose and said, "Chill and enjoy the rest of the house."

As I started to walk off Pharaoh called me back. 'Listen," he said, taking off his watch and handing it to me. "At 12 o'clock, I want you to come back here. Don't come in, just come to the door. I have a surprise for you. Now, go ahead." Pharaoh then pressed the intercom button on the wall and told Pasha to come see him. I could smell the scent of Pasha as she brisked by me on her way down the hall. Her sweet smell made her even more desirable. I thought to myself Pharaoh was too lucky to have a woman like that.

## Tune In Each Week to Urban Literary Review Radio

Executive Produced by
DC Bookdiva

Author Interviews
Industry News
Tips and Topics on Publishing

www.blogtalkradio.com/urbanliteraryreviewradio

And

## Street Reviews

www.youtube.com/streetreviews

# Order Form

DC Bookdiva Publications
#245 4401-A Connecticut Avenue, NW
Washington, DC 20008
www.myspace.com/dcbookdivapublications

**Name:** _____

**Inmate ID#** _____

**Address:** _____

**City/State:** _____ **Zip:**_____

| QUANTITY | TITLES | PRICE EACH | TOTAL |
|----------|--------|------------|-------|
| _____ | Up The Way, Ben | $15.00 | _____ |

## Coming Soon

| QUANTITY | TITLES | PRICE EACH | TOTAL |
|----------|--------|------------|-------|
| _____ | Draw | $15.00 | _____ |
| _____ | Keisha II-The Clit | $15.00 | _____ |
| _____ | A Killer's Ambition | $15.00 | _____ |
| _____ | Left Without A Choice | $15.00 | _____ |
| | **Sub Total** | **$** | _____ |

**Shipping/Handling (Via U.S. Media Mail) $3.95 1-2**

**Shipping** $ _____
**Total Enclosed** $ _____

**FORMS OF ACCEPTED PAYMENTS:**
Certified or government issued checks and money orders, all mail in orders take 5-7 Business days to be delivered. Books can also be purchased on our website at www.dcbookdiva.com and by credit card at 1866-486-8384.

Incarcerated readers receive 25% discount, Please pay $11.25 per book and apply the same shipping terms as stated above.

# STREET ELEMENTS
## THE ULTIMATE STREET MAGAZINE

#102

#103

#104

Street Elements magazine is an independent, quarterly published magazine based out of Tampa, Florida. Our goal is to focus on every "element" of the streets from Street Hustlers, sports, fashions, music, cars, etc. Street Elements prides itself with being an avenue for people from the streets to tell their story. We try to capture every element of what makes the streets a part of us. We strive to keep our readers happy by, supplying them with as much information as possible about the streets.
myspace.com/streetelementsmagazine

## Order Form

**Street Elements Magazine**
PO Box 11500
Tampa, FL 33680
www.streetelementsmag.com

Name: _____

Inmate ID: _____

Address: _____

City, State: _____ Zip: _____

| Quantity | Issue | Price | Total |
|---|---|---|---|
| _____ | Issue 102 | $14.00 | _____ |
| _____ | Issue 103 | $11.00 | _____ |
| _____ | Issue 104 | $ 9.00 | _____ |
| _____ | 1 Year Subscription | $25.00 | _____ |

Subtotal $_____

**Prices Include Shipping and Handling**

Total Enclosed $_____